CHARLOTTE LAMB

The Marriage War

D0012419

Harlequin Books

TORONTO • NEW YORK • LONDON
AMSTERDAM • PARIS • SYDNEY • HAMBURG
STOCKHOLM • ATHENS • TOKYO • MILAN
MADRID • WARSAW • BUDAPEST • AUCKLAND

ISBN 0-373-11913-5

THE MARRIAGE WAR

First North American Publication 1997.

This edition published by arrangement with Harlequin Books S.A.

® and TM are trademarks of the publisher. Trademarks indicated with ® are registered in the United States Patent and Trademark Office, the Canadian Trade Marks Office and in other countries.

Printed in U.S.A.

"Sancha, don't stop now.... You want it, I want it, we both need it— you know we do!"

He held out his hands; they were trembling slightly. "See that? That's how much I want you."

"As much as you wanted *her* the other night?" she asked bitterly, and he shut his eyes, groaning, turning away.

"Oh, not again! Do we have to bring that up again? Forget Jacqui!"

"I can't. Can you? Working with her every day, seeing her, being alone with her? You may not have slept with her—but you admit you almost did. Is she going to accept the end of the affair...?"

"We never had an affair!"

CHARLOTTE LAMB was born in London, England, in time for World War II, and spent most of the war moving from relative to relative to escape bombing. Educated at a convent, she married a journalist, and now has five children. The family lives on the Isle of Man. Charlotte Lamb has written over a hundred books for Harlequin Presents.

Books by Charlotte Lamb

ALSO AVAILABLE IN HARLEQUIN PRESENTS

SINS

1816—SECRET OBSESSION
1822—DEADLY RIVALS
1828—HAUNTED DREAMS
1834—WILD HUNGER
1840—DARK FEVER
1846—ANGRY DESIRE
1852—HOT BLOOD

CHAPTER ONE

THE morning the anonymous letter arrived was no different from any other Sancha had had over the past six years.

She had opened her brown eyes with a reluctant jerk when the alarm went off, hearing Mark stir in the twin bed beside hers before he stretched, yawning. For a second or two Sancha had fantasised about the years before the children started arriving, remembering waking up in a double bed, naked and sleepy, to find his hands wandering in lazy exploration. In those far-off, halcyon days they had usually made love in the early mornings as well as at night.

They had switched to twin beds a couple of years ago because she was always having to get up in the night, either to feed a baby or comfort a child, and Mark had complained about being woken whenever she left their bed. Sancha had often wished, since, that they had not stopped sharing a bed. They had lost their old, loving intimacy; making love could no longer be so spontaneous or casual, and since Flora's birth they'd rarely made love at all. At night Sancha was always too tired and in the mornings there was never time.

This morning she reluctantly pushed her memories aside and made herself fling back the duvet, her feet fumbling for slippers, groping her way into her dressing-gown. She rushed into the bathroom, cleaned her teeth, splashed cold water on her face, ran a comb through her curly red-brown hair and then began the job of waking the children. She didn't have to wake Flora, who was already bouncing noisily round and round her cot, stark naked, with her red hair in tangled curls around her pink face.

'I'm a kangaroo! Look at me, Mummy, I'm a kangaroo-roo-roo...'

'Lovely, darling,' Sancha said absently, retrieving the small nightdress from the floor and dropping it into the washing basket before picking Flora up with one arm and carrying her into the childrens' bathroom. 'Get up now!' she yelled into the room the two boys shared. Six-year-old Felix was still lying in bed, with his duvet pulled over his head. Five-year-old Charlie was up, pulling off his pyjamas with his eyes shut.

By the time Sancha had dealt with Flora and was heading for the stairs Felix was up, still yawning, and Charlie was in the bathroom. Sancha could hear Mark having his shower.

Downstairs, she scooped the letters and a daily newspaper off the front doormat, with Flora squirming under her arm, her dimpled legs in green dungarees kicking vigorously. Sancha disliked wasting money, so she had kept all Charlie's baby clothes, washed and neatly folded away in a drawer, in case another baby came along. It had saved a fortune. She hadn't needed to buy any new clothes at all and Flora looked great in them. The fashion for unisex baby clothes suited her.

Turning towards the kitchen, Sancha shouted back up the stairs to the two boys to hurry up or else. A sound of stampeding feet followed; at least they were both up.

Dropping the handful of letters and the newspaper onto the table, beside Mark's place, she pushed Flora into her highchair, handing her a spoon to bang, and then put the coffee percolator on.

She didn't bother to look through the letters—she rarely got any: just the odd postcard from a friend or relative who was abroad on holiday, brown envelopes from a wishful tax inspector who refused to believe she no longer earned any money, or offers from catalogues and firms trying to sell her something which came in envelopes marked urgently 'Open me and win a fortune!' She read the postcards, but the rest of her mail was usually discarded into the kitchen bin at once.

All Sancha's movements at this hour of the morning were automatic; she often felt like a robot, moving and whirling around the kitchen. She had so much to do and so little time to do it in that she had worked out long ago the fastest way to get the coffee percolating, the porridge cooking, slip a couple of croissants into the microwave to warm through, set out cups, cutlery and mugs of cold milk, pour the orange juice and spoon prunes into a bowl for Mark. All with the minimum of effort.

Hearing the crash of feet on the stairs, she turned off the porridge, poured it into the childrens' bowls, put the saucepan into the sink and ran cold water into it to make it easier to clean later, then grabbed Flora, who was climbing out of her highchair, and put her back into it just as Felix and Charlie tore into the kitchen.

Sancha caught them and checked that their faces and hands were clean, their teeth and hair brushed, their clothes all present and correct—Charlie often forgot important items, like his underpants or one sock. He was very absent-minded.

By the time Mark got down his children were all busy eating their breakfast. Flora beamed at him, showing him a mouthful of porridge and little pearly teeth. 'Dadda!' she fondly greeted him.

Mark looked pained. 'Don't talk with your mouth full, Flora!' He sat down and drank some of his orange juice, looking at his watch with a distracted expression. 'I'm going to be late. Hurry up, boys, we have to go soon.'

He ate his prunes while glancing through his mail. 'This is for you,' he said, tossing one envelope over to Sancha, his grey eyes briefly touching her then moving away, a frown pulling his black brows together.

She felt a sting of hurt over that look—had that been distaste in his eyes? Of course, at this hour, in her shabby old dressing-gown and no make-up, she wasn't exactly glamorous, but there was no time to do much about how she looked until he and the boys had left. She really must make more effort, though— it made her unhappy to have Mark look at her like that, as if he didn't love her any more. Her love for him was just as strong; she needed him.

To cover her distress, she picked up the white envelope. The name and address had been typed. 'I wonder who this is from?' she thought aloud, studying the postmark. It was local, which didn't help.

'Open it and find out,' Mark snapped.

What was the matter with him this morning? Hadn't he slept? Or was he worried about work? Sancha wished there was time to ask him, but Flora had knocked over her mug of milk. Sighing, Sancha mopped up the damage while Mark averted his gaze.

'None of the boys were this much trouble,' he muttered.

'You just don't remember, and she isn't really naughty, Mark. Just high-spirited.' Sancha wiped Flora's sticky face, kissing her on her snub nose. 'You're no trouble, are you, sweetheart?'

Flora leaned forward and gave her a loving bang on the forehead with her porridgy spoon, beaming. Sancha couldn't help laughing. 'Finish your breakfast, you little monkey!'

Mark got to his feet, looking out of place in this cosy, domestic room with its clutter of children, pine furnishings and cheerful yellow curtains. He was a big man, over six feet, with a tough, determined face and a body to match—broad shoulders, a powerful chest, long, long legs. His nature matched, too. People who had never met him before always gave him a wary look at first—he had an air of danger about him when he didn't smile, and he wasn't smiling now. He looked as if he might explode at any minute. He often had, over the last few months.

A pang of uneasiness hit Sancha—was Mark tired of family life after six years of babies? He was a man of tremendous drives; their sex life had been tumultuous before the children arrived, and Sancha missed those passionate nights. And his work as a civil engineer demanded a lot of energy, though he no longer spent so much time out on any of the sites where his firm were building. Mark was more often in the office now, planning, organising, working out on paper rather than physically, in the field, and she suspected he regretted the change in his working pattern. Did he also regret being married, having children, being tied down?

Curtly he said, 'Oh, by the way, I'll be late tonight.'

Sancha's heart sank. He was always being kept late at the office. 'What, again? What is it this time?'

'Dinner with the boss again. Can't get out of it. He wants to talk about the new development at Angels Field. We're running late on the schedule, and time is money.' But he didn't meet her eyes, and she felt another twinge of uneasiness.

Oh, no doubt she was imagining things, but her intuition told her something was wrong—what, though?

He turned away and said impatiently, 'Are you ready, boys? Come on, I can't wait any longer.' He always drove the boys to school, and Sancha picked them up again at three-thirty.

They clambered down from the table and headed for the door into the hall, but Sancha caught them before they could get away. 'Wash your hands and faces. You've got more porridge on your face than you got into your mouth, Charlie.'

Mark had gone to get the car. Sancha dealt with the boys and followed them to the front door, with Flora lurching along behind her.

'Try not to be too late,' Sancha called to Mark when the car drew up outside, and the boys got into the back seat and began doing up their seat belts.

Mark nodded. Early May sunlight gleamed on his smooth black hair; she couldn't see his eyes, they were veiled by heavy lids, but that air of smouldering anger came through all the same. What was the matter? Was something wrong at work? This weekend she must try to find time to sit down and talk to him, alone, once the children were in bed.

The car slid away; Sancha waved goodbye and stood in the porch for a few moments, enjoying the touch of morning sunlight on her face. It would soon be high summer; the sky was blue, cloudless, and there were roses out, and pansies, with those dark markings that looked like mischievous faces peeping from under leaves. The lilac tree was covered with plumes of white blossom which gave the air a warm, honeyed fragrance.

The house was a modern one, gabled, with bay windows on both floors. Detached, it was set in a large garden, with a low redbrick wall both front and back and a garage on one side. Mark's firm had built it for him when they'd got married, but they had a large mortgage and at times money had been tight— although it seemed easier now that Mark had been promoted and had a better-paid job. That meant working longer hours, however, and Sancha often wished he had fewer responsibilities.

Flora had taken the opportunity of her mother's absent-mindedness to sneak off into the garden, her eyes set on the yellow tulips edging the lawn.

'No, you don't,' Sancha said, pursuing her. 'We'll go for a walk when I've done all my jobs.' She picked her up, took another long look at the morning radiance of the garden and went back indoors, closing the door with one foot.

Her routine was the same every day. She worked in the kitchen first—cleared the table, piled dirty dishes into the washing-up machine and switched it on, sorted out the day's washing and put that into the washing machine to soak for half an hour—then carried Flora upstairs and dumped her into her cot while Sancha had a quick shower, herself, then dressed in jeans and an old blue shirt.

It was an hour later, when she had finished vacuum cleaning the sitting-room and hall, that she remembered the letter and went to the kitchen to find it. She made herself a cup of coffee, gave Flora a piece of apple to eat in her playpen, and opened the envelope. The letter was typed and unsigned. It wasn't very long; she read it almost in a glance, her ears deafened with the rapid bloodbeat of fear and jealousy.

Do you know where your husband will be to-night? Do you know who he'll be with? Her name is Jacqui Farrar, she's his assistant, and she has an apartment in the Crown Tower in Alamo Street. Number 8 on the second floor. They've been having an affair for weeks.

Sancha's heart lurched. She put a hand up to her mouth to stop a cry of shock escaping, caught the edge of her cup and knocked over her coffee. The hot black liquid splashed down her shirt, soaked through the legs of her jeans. She leapt up, sobbing, swearing.

'Naughty Mummy,' Flora scolded, looking pleasantly scandalised. Primly she added, 'Bad word. Bad Mummy.'

Sancha said it again furiously, looking for kitchen roll to do more of her habitual mopping up—only this time it was she who had made the mess, not Flora.

It can't be true, she thought; he wouldn't. Mark wouldn't have an affair. She would have known; she would have noticed.

Or would she? Yes! she thought defiantly, refusing to admit that her stomach was cramped with fear. He was her husband; she knew him. He loved her; he wouldn't get involved with anyone else.

But did he still love her? She remembered the distaste in his face that morning, over breakfast, and bit her lower lip. Mark no longer looked at her the way he used to; she couldn't deny that. Somehow, without her noticing it, love and passion had seeped out of their relationship, but that didn't mean there was anyone else. She couldn't believe he would be unfaithful to her. Not Mark. He wouldn't.

She had never met his assistant, although she knew the name. Jacqui Farrar had joined the firm only six months ago, from another civil engineering company. Mark had mentioned her a few times at first, but not lately.

Sancha had no idea what she looked like, even how old she was. It had never entered her head that there could be anything going on between her and Mark.

Of course there isn't! she told herself. Don't even think about it. Whoever had written that letter was crazy.

Sancha ran an angry hand over her tearstained face and then picked up Flora. At the moment they could never be apart, they were handcuffed together for all

Flora's waking hours—she could not be left alone for a second or she got into some sort of mischief.

Sancha often felt exhausted by the sheer, unrelenting nature of motherhood, longing for a few hours alone, a day when she did not have to think about other people all the time, when she could be lazy, sleep late, get up whenever she pleased or put on something more elegant than jeans, wear high heels, have her hair done, buy expensive make-up, shower herself with delicious French perfume—anything to feel like a woman rather than a mother.

But it was what she and Mark had wanted when they got married. They had talked about it from the start, in perfect accord in both longing for children. Mark had been an only child of older parents. His mother had been over forty when he was born, his father even older than that. Mark had had a lonely childhood and dreamt of having a brother or sister. His parents had died before he met Sancha; she'd never known them, but she had realised Mark's deep need to be part of a family at last. Sancha had been broody, too, had ached to have a baby, had seen herself as some sort of Mother Earth, creating this wonderful, close, warm family life, without any idea of how much work and sacrifice on her part would be involved.

Sighing, she popped Flora back into her cot, gave her a handful of toys to play with, then had another hurried shower and changed into clean jeans, a clean shirt. She stood in front of the dressing-table and studied herself bleakly. What did she look like? What on earth did she look like? A hag, she thought. I'm turning into a positive hag. No wonder Mark had given her a disgusted look this morning. She couldn't blame him. How long was it since she'd even thought about the way she looked?

Or had the energy to try to seduce Mark in bed, the way she once had, years ago, when they were first married? Once upon a time she would slide into bed naked and tease him with stroking fingers and soft, light kisses, but hold him off as long as possible, arouse him to a point of frenzy before she let him take her. They had been passionate lovers, hadn't they?

Biting her lip, she tried to remember when they had last made love, but couldn't. It must be weeks. A dull, cynical voice whispered to her. Months! It was months!

Since Flora's birth they had made love less and less often, and at first it had been she who had never felt like it. Mark had been gentle, sympathetic, under-standing; he hadn't got angry or complained. She had had three babies in six years; it wasn't surprising that she was so tired and listless.

They hadn't planned to have more than two children. Flora had been an accident, and that last pregnancy had been the worst. Sancha had had morning sickness, backache, cramp in her legs, restless nights—and even when she had had the baby she'd felt no better. She'd been too exhausted after being in labour for two days, in great pain much of the time. Afterwards she had kept crying; the changes in her hormones during and after her pregnancy had left her in emotional turmoil. A fit of the blues, her sister, Zoe, had called it. Her doctor had called it de-pression, but all Sancha knew was that the smallest thing could set her off on a crying jag and nothing seemed to help.

It hadn't lasted very long—a month or two, three at the most—but Flora, from the first moment of her arrival in the world, had been difficult; a restless, crying baby at night and in the daytime needing permanent attention.

Sancha had never really got back her energy, her enjoyment of life, her desire to make love. What energy she did have went into Flora and into her daily routine—the two boys, the house, the garden. Only now did she realise how little time she had spent alone with Mark over the past couple of years.

It had happened so gradually that she hadn't understood until now that they were drifting apart, inch by inch, hour by hour.

The jangle of the front doorbell made her jump. Who on earth could that be? She collected Flora and carried her back downstairs.

She was startled, and a little embarrassed, to find her sister standing on the doorstep. 'Oh, hello, Zoe,' she murmured, rather huskily. 'I thought you were filming in the Lake District this week?'

'We finished there yesterday so I drove back last night. I told you we were all going to be filming on location around here, didn't I? I've got a few days off before we start,' Zoe said, eying her shrewdly. 'Your eyes are pink—have you been crying?'

'No,' lied Sancha, wishing her sister was not so observant, did not see so much. Zoe had always been far too sharp and quick.

'Mummy swore,' Flora informed her aunt. 'Bad Mummy.'

'Bad Mummy,' agreed Zoe, watching Sancha. 'Who were you swearing at? The little love-bug, here? Having a bad day with her, or is something wrong?'

'I knocked my coffee over, that's all—no big deal,' Sancha said, but didn't meet her sister's thoughtful stare.

'Hmm.' Zoe grinned at Flora. 'Was it you who knocked Mummy's coffee over? I bet it was. Come to Auntie Zoe?'

Flora went willingly, and at once began to investigate the dangling, sparkly earrings Zoe was wearing.

'Hands off, monster,' Zoe told her, pushing her small pink hands down. 'Into everything, aren't you? Boy, am I glad I don't have any kids.'

'Time you had some,' Sancha said, getting a sardonic look from Zoe.

'Says who? You're no advertisement for the maternal state. Every time I see you, you look worse. How about a cup of coffee, or are you too busy?'

'Of course I'm not.' Sancha walked through into the kitchen and Zoe followed her. She was wearing what she no doubt thought of as 'casual' clothes— elegant, tight-fitting black leather trousers, a vivid emerald silk top. Sancha inspected them with envy. They were probably designer clothes, their cut was so good; they had 'chic' written all over them and had undoubtedly cost an arm and a leg.

She couldn't afford clothes like that—and even if she could she would never be able to wear them. Flora would ruin them in no time, would spill food on them, crayon all over them or be sick on them. Flora had a dozen charming ways of ruining clothes, and all without really trying. You couldn't accuse her of doing it deliberately.

They wouldn't look that good on Sancha, anyway. Zoe, however, was dazzling whatever she wore—a tall woman, already thirty-two, with flame-red hair and cat-like green eyes, beautiful, sophisticated, clever, talented and highly paid. She worked for a TV production company, and was currently making a four-part series of a bestseller novel with household names in the starring roles.

She had a small cottage outside town, but was barely there because her work took her all over the world. You never knew where she would be filming next. Last year she had worked on films in Spain and California. So far this year all her work had been back home, in the United Kingdom.

The sisters had always been very close, and since Sancha had got married they still saw a good deal of each other; Zoe was Sancha's closest friend, although their lives were so different.

Zoe's private life was usually as busy as her career. Sancha could not keep up with the men Zoe dated, often very starry, famous men, but none of them had ever been important enough for Zoe to introduce them to her sister, or her parents, which meant she'd never considered marrying them, or even setting up house with them. The only thing that mattered to Zoe seemed to be her career.

Before she'd met Mark, Sancha had been set on a career, too, but in photography, not films. She had been working for a top Bond Street photographer, specialising in the fashion business, and had had her eyes set on the heights. One day she'd meant to have her own salon, make her name world-famous. She had had dreams.

Mark's arrival in her life had changed all that. One minute she was focused entirely on her work—the next it didn't matter a damn to her. Only Mark mattered. She forgot everything but being with him, loving him, going to bed with him. He ate up her entire life.

Zoe had had very few problems in climbing to the top; her abilities were too outstanding and her personality too powerful. Sancha had grown up in her shadow, knowing she was not as beautiful or as brilliant. She might have been overshadowed by Zoe, lost confidence in herself—instead she had competed with her, in a perfectly cheerful way, had been determined to be as successful as her older sister, make her own name, become famous.

The competition between them had ended when Sancha got married and had children. She no longer cared about success, about beating Zoe; she was too happy to think about a career any more. In fact, the only time she touched a camera lately was to take pictures of her children.

Putting Flora into her highchair, Zoe opened the fridge and found some orange juice, poured a little into a mug and gave it to her, then sat down at the pine table, keeping a safe distance from her little niece and the possibility of getting splashed with juice.

Sancha made coffee, keeping her back to Zoe. 'How's the filming going? Smoothly, or are there problems?'

'Only one problem—the casting director insisted on picking Hal Thaxford.' Zoe's dry voice made Sancha

smile. She had heard her sister's views on Hal
Thaxford before.

'I know you don't like him—but he's quite a good
actor, isn't he?'

'He wouldn't know how to act his way out of a
paper bag. The man doesn't act. He just stands about
with folded arms, glowering like Heathcliff, or snarls
his lines.'

'He's sexy, though,' teased Sancha, getting down
the mugs and pouring the coffee the way Zoe liked
it—black and unsugared.

She almost dropped both mugs when she turned
and found Zoe reading the letter Sancha had left on
the table.

Zoe looked up and their eyes met. 'So that's why
you look like death warmed up.'

First white, then scarlet, Sancha snapped, 'How
dare you read my letters?'

Putting down the coffee so suddenly it spilled a
little, she snatched the letter from her sister.

Zoe was unrepentant. 'It was open; I couldn't help
seeing a few words. Once I'd done that, I had to know
the rest.' She stared at Sancha with sharp, narrowed
eyes. 'Is it true?'

Sancha sat down, pushing the crumpled letter into
her jeans pocket. 'Of course not!'

There was a little silence and Zoe frowned at her
sister, her face disbelieving. 'Did you recognise her
handwriting?'

Startled, Sancha shook her head. 'No.' Then she
thought briefly. 'What makes you think it was written
by a woman?'

Zoe's bright red mouth curled cynically. 'They always are. Men get at people in other ways. They either come right out with it, give you a smack, or they make funny phone calls...heavy breathing... whispered threats...that sort of thing. But women send poison pen letters, usually hysterical stuff about sex. Obviously this is from someone in Mark's office; maybe someone who fancies him herself, but never got a second look and is jealous of this assistant of his.'

Flora had drunk all her juice; she began banging her mug violently on her highchair tray. Zoe winced and took the mug away from her.

'How do you stand it all day long? It would drive me crazy.'

Sancha picked Flora up and carried her over to her playpen; Flora immediately picked up a toy elephant and crushed it lovingly to her.

'Mine effelunt,' she cooed. 'Mine, mine.'

Sancha ran a hand over the child's red curls. 'You know, she's just like you,' she told her sister, who looked indignant.

'Do you mind? I was never that over-active or exhausting.'

'Oh, yes, you were—Mum says you nearly drove her out of her mind. And you haven't really changed, either.'

Zoe contemplated her niece, who stared back then put out her small pink tongue, clutching the elephant tighter.

'Effelunt mine,' she said, knowing her aunt to be very well capable of taking the toy away from her.

'Monster,' Zoe said automatically, then asked a little uneasily, 'Is she really like me, or were you joking?'

'It's no joke. Of course she is,' Sancha told her, sitting down at the table again, and her sister shuddered before turning thoughtful eyes back to Sancha's face.

'So what are you going to do about this letter?'

Sancha shrugged, drinking some more of her coffee before saying, 'Ignore it, burn it in the Aga—that's where it belongs.'

'You're really sure it's a lie?' Zoe's eyes were shrewdly bright. She knew her sister far too well not to suspect she wasn't being entirely honest. Sancha's face, her eyes, her whole manner, were far too betraying.

Suddenly admitting the truth, Sancha gave a little wail. 'Oh, I don't know. It never entered my head until I got that letter, but it could be... We haven't been getting on too well for months, not really since Flora was born. First I was tired and depressed, and I couldn't...didn't want to. I don't know why—maybe my libido was flat after having three babies so close together. Mark was very good, at first, but it drifted on and on; we hardly talk, these days, let alone... It must be months since we...'

'Made love?' supplied Zoe when she stopped, and Sancha nodded, her face out of control now, anguished, tears standing in her eyes.

Zoe got up hurriedly, came round to put an arm round her, holding her tight.

'Don't, Sancha. I'm sorry. I didn't mean to upset you.'

Sancha pulled herself together after a minute, rubbed a hand across her wet eyes. Zoe gave her a handkerchief. She wiped her eyes with it and then blew her nose.

'Sorry.'

'Don't apologise, for heaven's sake!' Zoe exploded. 'In your place I'd be screaming the place down and breaking things, including Mark's neck! If you've been too tired to make love it's because of his children, after all! It takes two. They're as much his problem as yours. You'll have to tell him, Sancha, show him the letter—if it is a lie you'll know when you see his face, and if it's true he won't be able to hide that, either.'

Sancha looked at her bleakly. 'And then what do I do? If Mark tells me it's true and he's having an affair? How do I react to that? Do I say, Oh, well, carry on! I just wanted to know. Or do I give him some sort of ultimatum—me or her, choose now! And what if he chooses her? What if he walks out and leaves me and the children?'

'If he's likely to do that you're better off knowing now. You can't bury your head in the sand, pretend it isn't happening or hope it will all go away. Where's your pride, for heaven's sake?'

Anguish made Sancha want to weep, but she fought it down, struggled to keep her voice calm. 'There are more important things than pride!'

'Is there anything more important than your marriage?' Zoe demanded. 'Come on, Sancha, you've got to face up to this. Do you know...what was her name? Jacqui something? What's she like?'

'I've no idea; I've never set eyes on her.' Sancha's voice broke, her whole body trembling as she tried to be calm. 'Stop asking me questions. I need to think, but how can I think when there's so much to do all the time? Just keeping up with Flora drains all my energy.'

Zoe contemplated the two-year-old jumping round her playpen. 'I bet it does. Just watching her makes me feel drained.' She shot Sancha a measuring glance. 'Look, I have nothing much to do today. Why don't I stay here and look after Flora while you go off by yourself and think things over?'

Sancha laughed shortly. 'You'd be a nervous wreck in half an hour!'

'I've babysat for you before!'

'At night, when she was asleep—and not often, either. You have no idea what she's like when she's awake. You need eyes in the back of your head.'

Zoe shrugged. 'I'll manage; I'm not stupid. Off you go, forget about Flora for a few hours. Don't just moon about—do something about the way you look. Have your hair done! You haven't had a new hairstyle for years. That will make you feel a whole lot better. Don't worry about the boys; I'll pick them up from school. But can you be back by six because I've got a date at seven-thirty?'

Sancha hesitated a second or two more, then smiled at her sister. 'OK, thanks, Zoe—if you're sure...'

'I'm sure!'

'Well, thanks, you're an angel. I will have my hair done. You're right—I should. And if you have any real problems go to Martha—remember her? Lives across the street, only just five foot, with very short black hair? She'll help out if something does go wrong.'

Zoe grinned and nodded. 'OK, OK. Don't fret so much. Now scoot, will you, while the monster isn't looking.'

Flora was sitting with her back to them, struggling to force a small bear into one of her small plastic saucepans, far too absorbed to notice what was going on behind her.

Sancha gave her sister a grateful look, then grabbed up her purse and went out on tiptoe. Ten minutes later she was in her car, heading for the centre of town. First she went to the best hairstylist she knew, and managed to get an immediate appointment because someone had cancelled. The man who came to do her hair ran a comb through the thick curls with a grimace.

'This is going to take me for ever!' he groaned. 'Any ideas about how you want it to look?'

'Different,' Sancha said, feeling reckless. What she really wanted to say was, Make me beautiful, make me glamorous, help me get my husband back! If only she could switch back six years, to the way she'd looked before she'd started having babies and ruined her figure!

While the stylist began thinning and cutting her hair she leaned back in the chair with closed eyes, thinking. But she was still going round in circles, deciding first to do this, then that, and afraid of doing anything at all in case it precipitated a crisis which could lead to the end of her marriage.

The letter might be a hoax, a wicked lie. She could be torturing herself over nothing. But if it was true?

Her heart plummeted and she had to bite the inside of her lip to stop herself crying. What was she going to do? Was Zoe right? Should she confront Mark, show him the letter, ask him if it was true?

No, she couldn't—she was too scared of what might happen next. She felt as if she were standing in the middle of a minefield. Any step she took might blow everything up around her. The only safety lay in not moving at all. Not yet.

First she had to find out if there was any truth in the allegation. But how could she do that without asking Mark?

Tonight he was supposed to be having dinner with his boss, Frank Monroe, the man who had started the construction company and still owned the majority of the shares. Mark hadn't said where they were having dinner, but it was either at Monroe's house, a big detached place outside town, or at one of the more expensive restaurants.

She could ring Frank Monroe's house tonight and ask for Mark, make up some excuse about why she needed to talk to him. If Mark wasn't there she would know he had lied.

She sighed, and the stylist said at once, 'Don't you like it?'

Startled, she looked into the mirror and saw how much hair he had cut off.

Stammering, she hardly knew how to react. 'Oh . . . well . . . I . . .'

'It will look much better once I've blowdried it and brushed it into shape,' he promised. 'You can't see the full picture yet.'

'No,' she said with a wry twist of the lips. She could not see the full picture yet; she must wait until she could. But Zoe was absolutely right—she had to know the truth. She could not rest, now that the poison had been injected; she could feel it now, working away inside her, like liquid fire running through her veins.

An hour later she left the salon looking so different that she almost failed to recognise herself in the mirror. Her hair was now worn in a light mop of bright curls which framed her face and made her look younger.

Before her hair had been blowdried one of the young assistants had given her a facial and full make-up, using colours she would never have picked out for herself: a wild scarlet for her mouth, a soft apricot on her eyelids, a faint wash of pink blusher over her cheekbones. Then, while her hair was being blow-dried, she had had her nails manicured, but had refused to have them varnished the same colour as her mouth.

So the girl had painted them with clear, pearly varnish, and added a strip of white behind the top of each nail. That had given her fingers a new elegance, made them look longer, more stylish. Mind you, how long that would last, under the onslaught of Flora and the boys, the washing-up, the floor-polishing, the cleaning . . . who knew?

'You look great!' the assistants had told her as she'd paid her bill, and Sancha had smiled, knowing they weren't lying.

'Thank you,' she'd said, tipping them generously.

Walking along the main street of Hampton, the little English town an hour's drive from London, she saw the church clock striking the hour and realised it was now one o'clock. Only then did she remember that she hadn't eaten.

She would have lunch somewhere really exciting, she decided, feeling free and reckless. She walked along the High Street towards the best restaurant in town, a French bistro called L'Esprit, and began to cross the road—only to stop dead in her tracks as she recognised Mark on the other side. He had his arm around the waist of a girl he was steering towards the swing doors of the restaurant.

A car screeched to a halt behind her, its bumper inches away—the driver leaned out and yelled angrily at her.

'Are you crazy? I nearly hit you! What do you think you're doing? Get out of the road, you imbecile!'

Automatically apologising, her nerves frantic, Sancha hurried to the kerb and stood on the pavement, realising that Mark had gone into L'Esprit.

Who had the blonde been? A client? Sancha remembered Mark's arm around the girl's waist, his fingertips spread in a caressing fan.

The blonde had turned her head to look up into his eyes, saying something to him, her pink lips parted, their moist gleam sensual.

It's *her*, Sancha thought. She had never yet set eyes on Jacqui Farrar, but she was suddenly certain she had now seen her for the first time, and that it was true, the accusation in the anonymous letter. Mark had lied about what he was doing that evening. He wasn't having dinner with his boss—he was having it with Jacqui Farrar. They would go to her flat and . . .

Sancha took a deep, painful breath as her imagination ran ahead and pictured what Mark would be doing.

She wanted to stand there in the street and scream. She wanted to run into the restaurant, kill Mark. If she had a gun she would shoot him, or the blonde girl, or both of them. She wanted to hurt Mark as much as he had hurt her. She would like to go home and pull all his elegant, expensive suits out of the wardrobe and chuck them on the garden bonfire, watch them burn along with his beautiful designer shirts and silk ties. While she was wearing old jeans and shirts Mark was always beautifully dressed. He said it was necessary for his image as a top executive.

He frowned at her shabby clothes and unkempt hair, but he had never given her a personal allowance big enough to buy herself good clothes. Oh, he made her an allowance, but most of that money went on clothes for the children. They grew out of their clothes so fast, she was always having to buy them something, and there was never very much left over for her. No doubt that had never occurred to Mark; he left everything to do with the children to her, and never questioned what she did with the allowance he made her. If they went out together she always wore one of the outfits she had had for years, but which still looked smart. At least she hadn't put on much weight, but all her nice clothes were faintly out of date—not that Mark ever seemed to notice that.

But for a long time he had been looking at her with those cold grey eyes as if he despised her, was bored by her. She tried to remember when it had started— soon after Flora was born? No, not that far back.

Around the time Jacqui Farrar joined the firm? Her stomach cramped in pain. Yes, it must have been then.

The blonde couldn't be more than twenty-three; her figure hadn't been ruined by having three babies and her salary was probably good enough for her to afford tight-fitting, sexy clothes which showed off her figure. Mark had said once that she was clever, an efficient and fast-thinking assistant, but obviously it had not been the girl's brains that attracted him. Having seen her, Sancha was sure of that.

Sancha wanted to kill him. She hated him. Hated him so intensely that tears burnt behind her eyelids. Loved him so much that the possibility of losing him made her wish she was dead. There had never been anyone else for her; no other men before him had meant a thing. She had had a couple of boyfriends, but Mark had been the first man she'd fallen in love with, and for seven years Mark had been the breath of her being, the centre of her life. She could not bear to lose him.

I won't lose him, she thought fiercely. That little blonde harpy isn't getting him. He belongs to me.

CHAPTER TWO

SANCHA swung round and walked back along the High Street, not really seeing where she was going and with no idea of what she meant to do. She only knew she needed to think the situation through, and she couldn't bear to face Zoe until she had herself under control. Her sister would take one look at her face and know that something had happened—they knew each other too well; they had few secrets from each other. Zoe already knew about the anonymous letter, and it was typical of her that she should have read it; it would never have occurred to her that she had no right to read her sister's private mail.

There was one secret Sancha did not intend to share with Zoe. Zoe had asked her if she had any pride—oh, yes, she certainly did! She was far too proud to let anyone, even Zoe, see how much it hurt to know that Mark was unfaithful to her.

Again her dangerous imagination went haywire, sending her images of Mark with the blonde girl, kissing, in bed...

No! She would not think about that. That way madness lay. She would simply go out of her mind if she thought about Mark and that girl.

She opened her eyes and stared into a shop window. A dress shop. She tried to be interested in the dresses displayed on brightly smiling, stiffly posed mannequins. One dress did catch her eye, a jade-green shift dress with a little jacket—she loved that colour.

She leaned closer to look at the price ticket and her brown eyes opened wide. Heavens! She had never bought a dress that expensive.

Turning, she was about to walk on when she paused, frowning. It was so long since she had bought anything that pretty—why shouldn't she be extravagant for once? She was in a mood to do something reckless. And, anyway, Mark could afford to give her far more money than he did. He hadn't increased her allowance for ages, but now she thought of it he was always buying himself new shirts, new suits, new ties.

Taking a deep breath, she walked into the shop, and a woman turned to look her up and down, sniffing at her old jeans and well-washed shirt.

Her expression said that customers who dressed like Sancha were not welcome in her shop. A small, birdlike woman, with dyed blueish hair, she wore a pale beige dress that made her almost vanish into the tasteful pale beige décor of the shop.

'Can I help you?' she enquired in a chilly tone.

Sancha stood her ground, her chin up. She was in no mood to put up with this sort of treatment. Anyone would think that nobody ever wore jeans—but you only had to look along the street to see hordes of people wearing them. Maybe they never came into this shop? If they got this sort of treatment, Sancha could understand why.

'I want to try on the green shift dress in the window.'

The shop assistant did not like that. 'I'm not sure if we have it in your size,' she said icily, as if Sancha were the size of an elephant.

'The one in the window looks as if it would fit me,' Sancha said sharply, wanting to bite her, and maybe that showed in her face because, on hearing her size, the assistant reluctantly produced the dress and Sancha went into a cubicle to try it on.

It was a perfect fit. What was more, she loved it even more when she saw herself wearing it, so she got out her chequebook and bought it, although it made her nervous to see the price written down.

'I'll wear it,' she told the assistant. 'Could you give me a bag for the clothes I was wearing?'

Still not ready to thaw, the woman found a paper carrier bag and put Sancha's jeans and shirt into it with the air of someone who wished she had tongs with which to pick up the clothes. Her gaze flicked down to Sancha's feet; a sneer flitted over her face. Silently she conveyed the message that Sancha looked ridiculous in that stylish dress when she was wearing slightly grubby, well-worn track shoes.

She had a point. Sancha took the carrier bag and walked out of the shop. There was a shoe shop next door; she dived in there and bought some black high heels and a new black handbag that matched them. At least the girl in there was friendly, in her late teens, with pinky blonde hair and a lot of make-up on her face.

As Sancha paid for her purchases the girl said, 'I love that dress. You got it next door, didn't you? I saw it in the window.'

'So did I, but the old misery who runs the shop almost put me off. She looked at me as if I was something that had crawled out from under a stone. Is she always like that?'

The teenager giggled. 'Unless you have pots of money and she thinks you're upper class. She's a terrible snob. Take no notice of her. The dress looks wonderful on you.'

Sancha smiled at her gratefully. 'Thanks.' She needed a confidence-booster; her self-esteem had never been so low—practically on the floor.

She went on along the High Street, and was startled to get a wolf whistle from a window cleaner on a ladder who, when she looked up at him, gave her an enormous wink.

'Hello, beautiful, where have you been all my life?'

Sancha gave a nervous giggle and walked quickly off, but kept taking sidelong glances at her reflection in the shop windows she passed. Each time she felt a little shock of surprise; she hadn't yet got used to her new look—to the different hairstyle, the sleek green dress, the high heels which made her look taller, slimmer. It was surprising what a difference your appearance made to your whole state of mind. She had been going around feeling well-nigh invisible for years, as far as men were concerned. She didn't expect attention; she avoided it. She was too busy with her children and the housework; she had no time to think of herself at all.

It was very late now; she ought to find somewhere to eat before they stopped serving lunch. Spotting a wine bar, she dived into it and chose a light lunch of poached salmon, salad and a glass of white wine. She sat in a corner, where nobody could see her, and ate slowly, brooding over Mark. She had to decide what to do, but each time she thought about it she felt a clutch of agony in her stomach; her mind stopped working and pain swamped everything else inside her.

She drove home around two o'clock and found Zoe slumped on the sitting-room floor in a litter of toys, a look of dazed exhaustion on her face.

'Where's Flora?' asked Sancha, immediately anxious. Zoe groaned, running her hands through her hair.

'Asleep upstairs. I ran out of ideas to keep her occupied so I asked her what she wanted to do and she said she wanted a bath. It seemed like a good idea, so I took her up there and ran a bath, and she had a great time—drowning her plastic toys, making tidal waves and splashing me head to toe—but I got so bored I could scream, so I decided it was time she came out. That was when the trouble started. I picked her up and she yelled and kicked while I tried to dry her. I finally dropped her naked in her cot while I looked for some clean clothes, but when I turned round she was fast asleep, so I covered her with her quilt and sneaked off and left her. My God, Sancha, how do you bear it, day after day? Why aren't you dead?'

Sancha laughed. 'I sometimes think I am.'

Zoe gave a start, her eyes widening. 'Well, well,' she said, looking her over from top to toe. 'I only just noticed—you look terrific! I love the new hairstyle—you look years younger—and the dress is gorgeous. That should make Mark sit up.'

Sancha went a little pink, hoping she was right. 'Glad you approve. I don't know about you, but I'm dying for some tea. Did you eat?'

'After a fashion. I made a cheese salad for lunch; Flora ate some of the cheese and some tomato and celery, then threw the rest about until I took it away. Watching her eating habits put me off my own food so I didn't eat much, either, but I'd love a cup of tea and a biscuit. My blood sugar is very low now.'

They drank their tea in the kitchen; the warm afternoon silence was distinctly soporific and Sancha felt her eyelids drooping—Zoe seemed half-asleep too.

Zoe yawned, gave her sister a glance across the table, then asked, 'What have you decided to do?'

'Do?' Sancha pretended not to understand, but Zoe wasn't letting her off the hook.

'About Mark and this woman,' she said bluntly.

'I don't know. I haven't decided yet.'

'Show him the letter,' advised Zoe. 'Don't be an ostrich. You have to talk to him, Sancha.'

'I know. I will.' Sancha did not tell her that she had seen Mark, or mention the blonde girl. She knew she wouldn't be able to talk about it without breaking down, and if she did tell Zoe her sister would urge her to leave Mark or have a confrontation with him. Sancha needed more time to think.

Zoe finished her tea and looked at her watch. 'Do you feel up to collecting the boys, after all? Because I really need to go home and have a soak in the bathtub.' She gave her sister a comical look, rolling her eyes. 'I need rest and silence.'

'I know just how you feel. Flora is quite an experience—I shouldn't have left you with her,' Sancha said, smiling. 'Of course I'll get the boys—no problem.'

Zoe got up, stretching. 'I am completely whacked! You know, anyone who can cope with that little monster day after day has to be a superwoman. You're my hero.'

She kissed her on the top of her head and left, and Sancha sat in the kitchen with another cup of tea, listening to the silence in the house and grateful for it, hoping Flora would not wake up just yet. They had an hour before they had to collect the boys.

She had a bad feeling that the next few months were going to be the worst in her life. Zoe had been joking when she'd called her a superwoman—she only wished she was! But she wasn't. She was just a very ordinary woman in a very painful situation, and she did not really know what she was going to do. She only knew she loved her husband deeply, and couldn't bear the thought of losing him.

But she couldn't bear, either, the idea of him with another woman. That was eating at her, driving her crazy.

What was she going to do?

That evening she put the boys and Flora to bed at their usual time, after feeding them one of their favourite suppers—a horrifying mix of scrambled egg and baked beans on toast which Charlie had invented one evening and which they had kept demanding ever since. She gave them some fruit, after that, and plain vanilla ice-cream.

Sancha had not eaten with them. She could never really enjoy a meal eaten with her children. Her digestion couldn't cope with the constant getting up and down, the nervous tension of watching Flora carefully drop beans on the floor, or the two boys kicking each other under the table.

She often did eat with them, of course, but it was never a pleasure. Tonight she had decided to wait until they were in bed and then heat herself some soup. She wasn't hungry.

By the time she had finished her soup and a slice of toast there was silence upstairs. The children were all fast asleep. Sancha curled up in front of the electric log fire and ate an apple, staring into the flickering flame effect of the fire and brooding on Mark and his woman.

She wished she knew if he was with the blonde tonight, or if he was genuinely having dinner with his boss. Her eye fell on the telephone and she jumped up, picked up the telephone book which lay beside it, and began flicking through the pages. She found Jacqui Farrar's name quite quickly, stared at the number, hesitated, then on an impulse dialled it.

The phone rang and rang; she was about to hang up when the ringing stopped and a low, husky voice slurred, 'Yes?'

Sancha couldn't think what to say.

'Hello? This is Jacqui Farrar,' the voice at the other end said.

Sancha was still silent, wanting to hang up but transfixed, listening to the voice of this woman who might be her husband's mistress.

'Hello? Hello?' the other woman said, and then, in the background a man's voice spoke.

'Is there anyone on the line? Can you hear breathing? Here, give me the phone. Those pests make me sick. I'll get rid of him for you.'

It was Mark's voice. Sancha's heart hurt as if a giant hand were squeezing all the life-blood out of it.

A second later he was snarling in her ear. 'Look, you creep, get off this line and don't—'

Sancha put the phone down and stood there, eyes closed, trembling. It was all true. He was there, now, with Jacqui Farrar. Had they already made love, or were they going to?

No, she couldn't bear to think about it.

She turned off the electric fire and the lights, closed all the doors, going through her nightly routine with the dull plodding of a robot, moving heavily, not seeing anything around her because her mind was so possessed with unbearable images. She wished she could shut them all off, like the television; she wished she could stop the pictures coming, but she was helpless in the grip of jealousy and pain.

She would never sleep tonight, but tomorrow she would have to go through the usual round of duties— taking care of the children, doing the housework, the shopping, the cooking. Well, that would be easier than sitting around with nothing to do but brood. She would try to keep busy, try not to have time to think.

She was still awake when Mark got home. She heard the car purr slowly up the drive into the garage, then a few minutes later the front door opened and closed quietly. Sancha sat up on one elbow and looked at the green glow of the alarm clock—it was nearly one in the morning. He had been with that woman all this time.

She lay down again, staring up at the ceiling, listening to Mark moving about downstairs. The fridge door opened and shut; he was probably getting himself a glass of iced water to drink if he woke up in the night.

He began coming upstairs. She would know his footsteps if she were dead, and knew which stair he stood on by the muted creaking. He was trying not to wake her. He didn't want her to know he was coming home at that hour. He didn't want to answer any questions about where he had been, what he had been doing until this time of night.

He was trying to get away with it, betraying her and their marriage but unwilling to pay the price, face the consequences.

Well, he was going to have to! She was going to take Zoe's advice and confront him, tell him she knew and he could stop lying. Either he stopped seeing his girlfriend or their marriage was over.

Holding her breath, she waited for him to open their bedroom door and come into the room, but he didn't. He walked on past and went into the little spare bedroom at the end of the corridor.

It was like a blow in the face. He wasn't even going to share her room tonight—maybe not any other night!

Of course, he had slept in the spare room before—when she'd first come home from hospital with Flora he had slept elsewhere because of the constant interruption during the night, when the new baby woke up yelling for food or attention. But that had only been for the first couple of weeks. When the new twin beds had been delivered Mark had rejoined her in this room.

Rage suddenly exploded in Sancha's head. She jumped out of bed and ran down the corridor, bursting into the spare room just as Mark was getting into bed.

He was naked. The angry, accusing words froze on Sancha's lips. She hadn't seen him naked for months. When you had children you didn't wander about without any clothes on, and they hadn't been making love. Now her heart began to race, and her ears were deafened with the sound of her own blood rushing round her body.

She couldn't take her eyes off that powerful, lean body; he was intensely masculine, with a muscled width of shoulder and deep chest, dark, rough hair curling down towards the strong thighs and long legs.

Her mouth went dry. She had not felt this intense desire for so long she almost didn't know what was happening to her. Heat began to burn deep inside her; she could scarcely breathe.

'Did I wake you up? Sorry, I tried to be very quiet,' Mark said curtly, looking away with that frown of irritation, and slid between the sheets, pulling them up to his neck as if to hide his nakedness from her, as if he disliked having her look at him.

She swallowed, fighting a longing to go over and touch him, run her hand down over that strong male body; she would have given anything to get into bed with him and caress him but she didn't dare risk a rejection. 'Why are you sleeping in here?'

'So I shouldn't wake you, obviously,' he said, sardonic and offhand. He wasn't even looking at her now. He had his eyes fixed on a space beside her. She realised he did not want to see her; her presence in the room was an embarrassment to him. There was a trace of dark red along his cheekbones and his jawline was tightly clenched.

'I *am* awake now,' she said fiercely, the pain of his indifference stabbing at her. 'Why were you so late? Where were you tonight, Mark?'

He snapped, 'I told you. Having dinner with my boss.' Then he carefully yawned, not a very convincing performance. His face and body were too tense to be relaxed enough for sleep. 'Look, I'm tired— we'll talk in the morning. I might as well sleep here tonight, now I'm in bed.' He leaned over and switched off his bedside lamp. 'Goodnight, Sancha.'

Angry words seethed inside Sancha's head, almost came out of her in a hot gush, but the habit of years took over. Since the birth of her first child she had learned to take second place, to accept the way things were, not to fight the inevitable. Mothers had to; the self had to step back for a while, let the child take precedence over any personal needs or desires. She wanted to scream at Mark, but she forced her rage down, drew breath, very quietly closed the door—although she wanted to slam it, she mustn't wake the children—and walked back along the landing somehow. She wasn't sure how she kept one foot moving in front of the other.

In the bedroom she sank down on her bed, shaking so much she felt as if she were falling to bits. The scream was trapped in her throat; she felt it trying to come out, put her balled fist into her mouth to silence it and bit down on her knuckles. Bit until she felt the saltness of her own blood seep into her mouth.

How dared he? How dared he talk to her in that brusque voice, look at her with such cold, remote eyes? When he was lying to her, betraying her with another woman? Well, he needn't think he was getting away with it. She knew what he was up to—it was some sort of male power game. Typical of them, utterly typical—shifting the blame, trying to make it look as if it was *she* who was in the wrong, *she* who was behaving badly, not him, never him.

Their sons did it all the time—played the same game, put up the same instinctive defence. 'Me? Mum, you don't think I'd do that. I didn't—not me—it wasn't me. It must have been Flora who spilt the milk,

tore the comic, broke the cup, ate the chocolate...'
Or any of the hundred tiny crimes committed in this
house every day while Sancha was cast in the role of
detective, judge and jury all in one, trying hopelessly
to pin the blame on one of her children while suspecting all of them. The boys always tried to accuse
Flora, but if she was asleep in her cot and couldn't
be proved guilty they turned on each other, both
equally full of righteous indignation and wide-eyed
innocence.

But they were children. Mark was a grown man.
He needn't think he was getting away with anything.
She would talk to him tomorrow morning, before the
children woke up.

She set her alarm for half an hour before she needed
to get up, but when she went along to wake Mark the
spare room was empty. He must already be up. Sancha
ran downstairs, but he wasn't there, either. He had
left the house while she was asleep.

There was a note on the kitchen table. She snatched
it up and read it hurriedly. 'Had to get to work early.
Mark.'

She screwed the paper up and threw it across the
room, sobbing with pain and anger.

He was lying; she knew it. He had left to avoid
facing her. He had sensed she was going to ask
awkward questions and didn't want to answer them.

But he was going to. Sooner or later he was going
to have to talk to her.

Later in the morning she and Flora set off to the small
neighbourhood shopping centre and were heavily
laden by the time they ran into Martha Adams, the
only neighbour who was really friendly with Sancha.

She stared, grinned. 'You've had your hair done! Marvellous! You look years younger—suits you shorter.'

'Thanks. I feel lighter, too.'

Martha contemplated Sancha's three shopping bags. 'Been on a buying spree?'

'It's just food,' Sancha groaned. 'The boys eat an incredible amount every day. Between them and Flora we went through half a box of cornflakes this morning alone. I can only just keep up with them.'

'Come and have a coffee,' invited Martha, and they walked across the street to the Victorian Coffee House, which had been built a year earlier to look around a hundred years old.

The waitresses were all young and pretty, and wore Victorian black and red print dresses with starched caps and aprons. The menu was couched in Victorian language, too. Sancha and Martha didn't need to read it; they had been there before and knew the menu by heart.

Martha ordered what they always had. 'Two coffees, two hot buttered muffins and hot chocolate with a marshmallow on top for the little girl.'

'You got it,' said the waitress, and vanished with a swish of long skirts.

Flora had spotted the Victorian rocking-horse which was one of the major attractions of the place for her. For once there was no other child riding it.

'Want a ride, want a ride,' she began to chant, trying to climb down out of the highchair Sancha had popped her into.

Martha lifted her out and carried her over to the rocking-horse. Flora at once began to gallop, crowing with delight.

Sancha watched her with fierce love; Flora was demanding, exhausting, but above all adorable, and Sancha would die to protect her. Yet by one of fate's strange ironies it had been Flora's birth that had driven Sancha and Mark apart.

It wasn't that Mark didn't love the child or hadn't wanted her—more that by needing her mother's full-time attention Flora had driven a wedge between her parents, had soaked up so much of Sancha's time and care that there had been nothing left for Mark.

While Sancha watched her child Martha had been watching Sancha, her forehead creased.

'Is something wrong?'

The question made Sancha start. Only then did she realise she was on the point of tears again. It kept happening since she'd got the anonymous letter. Turning her head away, she brushed a hand across her eyes.

'No, of course not,' she lied, forcing a smile as she turned back to face Martha's intent gaze.

Just five feet tall, and built on a diminutive scale to match, with a slender body and short legs, Martha had a mobile, heart-shaped face and bobbed black hair without a trace of grey yet—although she was forty years old. She lived alone in the house across the street from Mark and Sancha and her home was a magnet for all Sancha's children because Martha kept a cat and two dogs—sleek red setters, with gleaming manes and liquid dark eyes.

Her eyes shrewd, she refused to accept Sancha's lie. 'Come on, you know you can talk to me. I won't repeat anything you tell me,' she murmured, with one eye on Flora. 'Having problems? Not Flora?'

Sancha laughed. 'Flora's always a problem!'

'That's true,' Martha said, smiling. 'But there is something wrong, isn't there? Is it the boys? Or Mark?'

Her quick ears caught Sancha's faint, quickly suppressed sigh.

'It's Mark?' Martha deduced immediately. 'He isn't ill? Or is it his job? Is he having trouble at work?'

Sancha gave her a wry look. 'What a little Sherlock Holmes you are! It's nothing. Forget it.'

Martha studied her face. 'You look terrible—did you know that? As if you haven't slept a wink all night. You seemed fine last time I saw you—when was that? Couple of days ago? Nothing was wrong then. So what's happened since?'

Sancha glanced at Flora's small, wildly rocking body. Flora was oblivious of everything going on around her, could not hear their lowered voices, anyway.

It was tempting to talk to Martha, who had been the first neighbour to visit them when they had moved into the newly built house across the street from her, bringing a plate of home-baked biscuits and a bunch of roses from her beautiful garden. She had been a rock during the years since—had done the shopping for Sancha whenever she couldn't get out, babysat, been ready to listen to Sancha's problems with the children and given advice and practical help whenever she could.

Sancha had always felt very lucky to have such a good neighbour, and she, in her turn, had tried to be very supportive to Martha during her own time of trouble, when Martha's schoolteacher husband, Jimmy, had run off with an eighteen-year-old he had been teaching at the nearby college. Their elopement had caused a scandal and the local newspapers had been full of the story; reporters had badgered Martha, waited outside her house for her to emerge, called questions through the letterbox, and photographers had rushed to get snatched photos of her if she came out.

After a day of this Sancha had smuggled Martha into her own home under cover of night, and Martha had stayed in the spare room until the hoo-ha died down. The depth of their friendship had really begun during those days; Sancha had been the one person Martha had felt able to talk to, freely, and she had never broken Martha's trust.

She knew she could trust Martha now. After a brief hesitation, she muttered, 'Well, actually, I am a bit upset... I... got a poison pen letter yesterday.'

Martha frowned distastefully. 'A poison pen? Chuck it in the fire and forget whatever it said, Sancha. Only sick people write them.'

'I know,' Sancha said bitterly. 'But I think this one was telling the truth—it said Mark is having an affair.'

'Oh...no...' Martha looked at her with disturbed eyes. 'I don't believe it. Mark loves you! Take no notice, Sancha...'

'I wouldn't have—I hadn't suspected anything—but I'm afraid it...' Her voice shook and she paused, fixedly watching Flora, who was still chanting and rocking rhythmically. 'It's true,' she went on huskily. 'The letter said he was going to be with his assistant last night. He'd told me he was having dinner with his boss. I rang her apartment and he was there; I heard his voice.' Distress made her voice quiver. 'And earlier, I saw them together—in town, having lunch. I'd never seen her before, but I'm sure it was her. And

Mark had his arm round her waist. Oh, Martha she's so young...beautiful, blonde...and about fifteen years younger than Mark. I felt sick just looking at her. She was wearing wonderful clothes and had the sort of figure men flip over.'

Martha had listened intently, frowning. 'Oh, Sancha...I'm so sorry... You tackled Mark? What did he say?'

'I haven't had a chance—he didn't get home last night until after midnight, and this morning he left before I got up. With the children around all the time it's difficult to talk to each other, anyway. I'll have to wait until they're asleep tonight.'

Martha nodded. 'Oh, you mustn't talk about it when the children are in earshot.'

Sancha gave a long sigh. 'And it's Friday today. If I don't get a chance to talk to him tonight the children will be at home all day tomorrow and Sunday. It will be impossible to be alone.'

'How would it be if I took all three of them to the zoo tomorrow?'

Sancha took a deep, painful breath. 'Oh, Martha...would you?'

Martha smiled. 'I'd love to. We could have lunch, spend all day out. The weather is so good it would be perfect—and I always enjoy spending time with your kids.' She glanced round at Flora, lowered her voice to a thready whisper. 'Sancha, don't let your marriage break up without fighting to save it. I wish to God I hadn't been so quick to divorce Jimmy. He might have come back to me after he split with that girl. It was just a crazy fling; he lost his head for a while. But it didn't last a year. I was so hurt and angry that I went ahead with the divorce anyway, because

I couldn't stand the loss of face—everyone knowing he had dumped me for a kid half my age. I wanted to hit back. Now I often wish I hadn't.'

Sancha looked at her with sympathy, with anxiety. Why was life always so complicated, so fraught with problems? Like walking on eggshells; you could hear them break at every step you took. If only it was easier to see ahead and know the consequences of what choices you made!

Martha said gently, 'Don't make my mistake. I'd give anything to start again, give Jimmy another chance, but it's too late. He wrote to me a couple of times, begging me to meet him, talk to him, but I wrote him a very bitter letter telling him to get lost. After that he emigrated to Australia and I haven't heard from him since. If you love Mark, don't be too hasty in making any decisions. Whatever happens, wait—and make sure your marriage is really over before you think about divorce.'

CHAPTER THREE

MARK did not get home that night until after eight o'clock, by which time the children were all in bed, asleep, and Sancha was sitting in the living-room, curled up on the carpet in front of the electric fire, brooding. In winter she would have had the central heating switched on, but not in May, when the temperature kept rising; it would be midsummer in a few weeks. This had been a warm day, but now that night had fallen the temperature had dropped with it. Sancha had been feeling chilled and bleak all day, knowing that she had to talk to Mark when he got home, but as the time had ticked past and he had not come she hadn't been able to stop shivering.

It had still been daylight when she'd sat down with a cup of coffee after picking at a little of the salad she had made to go with the grilled chicken which she had intended to cook for Mark's supper. Slowly the light had waned, and now the room was shadowy where the red glow of the fire did not reach.

When she heard the car she sat upright, her body tense, listening to Mark driving into the garage, closing the doors, walking to the front door and using his key. The front door opened and shut, she heard him take off his coat and hang it up, then he entered the room behind her.

'Why are you sitting in the dark?' He switched the light on and she flinched from it.

Without looking round, she asked, 'Why didn't you let me know you would be late again?'

'I'm sorry. I was about to leave at the usual time when there was an emergency out on the Bailey Cross Road site—an excavator went out of control, a couple of men were injured. I had to drive out there so that I could make a report.'

'You could have rung me!'

'I thought it would only take half an hour but it was much worse than I'd thought. It took much longer.'

'You have a mobile phone in your car!'

'Yes, but...'

'But you never even thought of ringing me to warn me! I'm the last person on your mind these days, aren't I?'

She was on her feet by now, looking at him with bitter resentment, yet still remembering to keep her angry voice low so as not to wake the children.

He flushed staring back at her, his long body tense, and she thought, irrelevantly, stupidly, that he had not yet even noticed her new hairstyle, or that she was wearing the new jade-green dress instead of her usual jeans. But then he never really saw her any more, did he?

'I've said I was sorry!' he muttered. 'I'd have rung you if I'd had the time, but as soon as I arrived I had to deal with a dangerous situation. The excavator had hit a car, which caught fire, and there was a burst water main. The site foreman was one of the injured men and the other men were running around in a panic, not knowing what on earth to do... The firemen had only just arrived—it was utter chaos. OK, I admit, the last thing on my mind was ringing to let you know I'd be late for dinner, but in a situation like that you just go on automatic pilot; you forget minor details.'

'Oh, thanks!' she snapped. 'So that's what I am to you—a minor detail!'

Mark gave a low snarl, his hands clenching at his sides. 'What the hell is the matter with you lately?'

Sancha was angry enough by then to swing round and pick up the anonymous letter, which she had been reading again by firelight earlier, and which lay on the carpet beside her empty coffee-cup.

She held it out to Mark, who frowned, taking it. 'What's this?'

Her voice shook. 'Read it and find out.'

He unfolded the slightly grubby sheet of paper which she had been carrying around in her pocket all day. She watched him read it, saw the shock hit him, the tightening of his whole face, the tension in jaw and mouth, the hard narrowing of his grey eyes.

'God!' he muttered, then looked up rather sharply. 'Did it come through the post? Where's the envelope?'

'I threw it away.'

He gave her an irritated look. 'For heaven's sake—why on earth did you do that?'

'I don't know...I suppose...' She suddenly wanted to hit him. 'Stop bullying me! I usually throw envelopes away—why shouldn't I?'

'Isn't that obvious? It would have given us a clue to who sent it!'

'I thought of that. Do you think I'm stupid? It was typed. There were no clues to who had sent it.'

'Local postmark?'

She burst out in pain. 'Never mind who sent it— is it true?'

Mark crumpled the sheet of paper and threw it across the room, then ran a hand over his face as if to expunge the betraying traces of reaction from it while he worked out how to answer her.

Bitterly Sancha said, 'It's a simple question, isn't it, Mark? Is it true or not? Are you having an affair with your assistant? Don't stand there working out what to say—just tell me the truth.'

He turned away and walked across the room, his dark head bent, pushing his hands into his pockets. Sancha waited, watching the long, supple line of his back under the smooth jacket, remembering that glimpse of him naked the other night, how her body had burned, how she had lain sleepless for hours afterwards, tortured by desire and grief. She was fighting the same pain now, because she knew, she was certain, the letter's allegations were true. If they had been lies he would have reacted in a very different way—would have laughed, or been angry, would have said something, not turned away and stood there in silence, unable to look at her.

'Why, Mark? Why?' she cried out, and he swung round then to look at her, his face darkly flushed, his eyes glittering like ice, like jagged diamonds that could cut and wound.

'Why?' he repeated. 'Why?' Then, unbelievably, he laughed—a deep, harsh, angry laughter that made her flinch as if he had hit her. 'You really don't know? If that's true, it's because you don't give a damn about me. I sometimes wonder if you ever did.'

'How can you say that? You know I . . .' she whispered, cut to the quick, and couldn't go on, too choked with emotion.

'I know I was necessary to the way you wanted your life to work out! You needed a man to give you children, a home, and now you have them you don't need me any more. I'm superfluous, except for the money I bring home to pay for all of this!' He gestured angrily around the room, at the deep-piled carpet, the comfortable furniture. 'My money makes your cosy life with the kids possible, doesn't it? Just a pity you have to take me with it.'

She opened her mouth to tell him that it wasn't true, any of it, that she loved him, she always had—but he swept on fiercely, looking at her as if he hated her.

'You've made it very obvious that you wish I'd just vanish. You hardly even look at me or talk to me these days, and as for sex—how long is it since we slept together? Can you even remember? Come on, think about it—since Flora was born, how many times have we made love?'

The onslaught had made her so nervous that when he took a long stride towards her she backed, her nerves jumping.

He stopped, a few inches away, his eyes flashing. 'Oh, don't worry, I'm not about to rape you! I have too much self-respect to force myself on a woman who doesn't want me! That's why I haven't tried to get into your bed all these past months—although you can count the times we've slept together this year on the fingers of one hand! We aren't having a marriage, Sancha—we're just living under the same roof. And I'm sick of it, sick of being ignored and cold-shouldered.'

Tears burst behind her lids. 'Mark! How can you say that? I've never cold-shouldered you!'

'It felt damned cold whenever I tried to get into your bed and you pretended to be asleep, or too tired to make love,' he ground out between his teeth.

'I wasn't pretending. I'm always tired by the evening—looking after three children and running a house isn't a picnic, you know!' she threw back defiantly, then softened, held out a hand to him, pleading, 'Mark, I'm sorry if I've hurt you somehow . . . it never occurred to me that you were thinking I didn't love you any more. Why didn't you talk to me before? Why didn't you say something?'

'You don't think I was going on my knees to get my own wife to take some notice of me?' he snarled. 'I've got some pride left! Well, OK. You don't want me any more, so why should it matter a damn to you if I've found someone else?'

Sancha felt the admission like a stab to the heart. He was watching her with fixed, intent eyes, as if waiting to see the blow go home, so she fought the pain, swallowing until she could speak. Then she asked through lips that trembled, 'Are you in love with her?'

His face tightened even more, the lines of his cheekbones so sharp they seemed to be coming through his pale skin.

'I'm not discussing Jacqui with you!' he said after a second, in a biting tone. 'We're talking about you, Sancha, you and me—not Jacqui. If we had had a real marriage, this past couple of years, you'd know exactly what was going on in my life—you wouldn't need to pick up clues from anonymous letters. We never talk to each other, do we? If I try to talk, you never listen—you're too engrossed in your children!'

Stung, she threw back, 'They're your children, too!'

He nodded, pushing his dark hair from his face with a raking, impatient gesture. 'Yes, and I love them— but I'm not obsessed with them. I have room for other things in my life. You've made it very clear that they always come first with you, that nothing but them matters as far as you're concerned. Certainly not me.'

She looked at him with widening, incredulous eyes. Was he jealous of the children? Of his own children? 'But . . . they have to come first at the moment, Mark! They're so young; they need me twenty-four hours a day. I'm on my feet all day long, running around after them—especially Flora, you know how demanding she is! By the time you get home I'm exhausted, I'm like a zombie. I just want to flop out somewhere and sleep like the dead.'

'Every night, Sancha? Every damn night?'

The harsh tone made her shiver, and she moved closer to him, touched his arm, only to have him jerk away from her.

Softly she pleaded, 'Mark, please . . . it won't be like that for ever! Just while they're small and need me all the time.'

'And how long will that be? How long, Sancha? How much longer will it go on like this? One year? Two? Six? Ten? How long do you expect me to wait around on hold for you to remember I exist?'

The question was rhetorical; he didn't wait for an answer, his eyes raking her face with a bitter stare that was like being struck.

'No, of course not! Now I know . . . realise . . . Mark, I didn't suspect you felt this way . . .' she began huskily, but he talked over her, his voice hard and angry.

'I know you didn't! You haven't noticed me at all for months. If you had, you'd have seen that I had problems and needed help—needed your support, a little human comfort.'

She was taken aback, frowning. 'What do you mean—problems? What problems?'

His mouth twisted in cold sarcasm. 'Don't pretend to be interested now! You're too late with a show of sympathy.'

What was he talking about? She looked at him blankly, trying to guess what had been wrong—what hadn't she noticed, apart from not suspecting that he was getting involved with someone else? Her female instincts rapidly leapt to a conclusion. If he were one of the children, who seemed to be moody and out of sorts, she would immediately suspect some health problem—was that it?

'Are you ill?' she asked anxiously, studying him even more closely, trying to read some clue in the way he looked. He hadn't always been this thin, had he? Had he lost weight lately? The suit didn't fit quite perfectly now; the waistband was a little slack, the material hung loose in places.

She should have noticed; why had she missed the signs? Maybe he was right? Maybe in being so concerned with her children she had forgotten her husband? But he had never been ill that she could remember.

Mark had always been very fit. He spent so much time in physical work—tramping around the sites, climbing ladders, shifting bricks and timber, working with his hands, using his muscles. He was a tough, very powerful man who had almost never had a day's illness in his life.

Now that she looked at him closer, though, she saw how drawn and tense his features were—the set of his cheekbones more angular, his jaw clenched as if in pain, the line of his mouth weary. Even his skin had a greyness, a pallor that she had never seen before. What could be wrong?

Her imagination ran riot, conjuring up the worst possible illnesses. Oh, no, she thought, turning pale herself—not cancer. Please, God, not cancer.

'No, I'm not ill,' he snapped. 'Do I look ill? I've always been as fit as a flea. I suppose I've lost a little weight lately, but that's because I've lost my appetite and I've been worried. There's nothing physically wrong with me.'

Colour came back slowly into her face and she breathed more easily. 'What have you been worried about, Mark?' she asked quietly.

He hesitated, then said in an offhand voice, 'Well, you might as well know. It affects you too. It's the company—we're under attack. Grainger—you know Grainger, he heads GRO Construction, the big national company that are always advertising on TV?'

She nodded, a vague memory coming back of seeing the man on television, fronting one of his adverts. A heavy man in his fifties with a false smile and eyes like gimlets. 'I remember him.'

'Well, Grainger is into expansion at the moment, and we're one of the smaller companies he's targeting. He's been buying up the shares whenever any came on the market, building a share base in the company. It was a while before we realised a take-over was in the wind, and we've been fighting to stop it ever since—that's why I've had to work late so often these last weeks.'

At once she thought with a sick relief, Oh, then he hasn't been with *her* every time he was late? He really has been working; he hasn't been lying all this time.

'Is it OK now?' she asked hopefully. 'Did you win?'

He grimaced. 'I wish to God we had—but we don't know what's going to happen. Grainger has issued a share offer. Our shareholders will have to decide whether to accept one of his shares in exchange for two of ours.'

Frowning, Sancha asked, 'Is that a good offer?' She had no idea about the way the business was run, or what value the company's shares had. She wished now she had taken more interest. She might then have realised that Mark had worries on his mind.

He shrugged. 'It's going to be tempting for the shareholders. Yes. His company is much bigger than ours, and has been going far longer. Frank and I have been putting together our counter-offer, which will go out to all the shareholders next week. We're promising them a good dividend if they stick with us, and painting a rosy picture of the future. A few days after that there'll be a shareholders' meeting, and then they'll vote—a postal vote. Until those votes are counted we have no idea what the future holds for us.'

Nor did Sancha. She was listening to what he told her, intently, because what happened to his company mattered to her, too—all their lives were dependent on it. Oh, she should have taken more interest before. Why had she left all that to him? Why hadn't she got him to talk to her about his work? Yet, although the surface of her mind was occupied with that, underneath she was eaten alive with personal problems, with questions about the other woman—the woman he wouldn't even discuss with her.

Does he discuss me with her? Do they talk about me together in bed? Does he complain about me to her?

Each question was a turn of the knife Mark had stuck into her; she felt she was bleeding to death internally.

Sancha hated her, this blonde girl so much younger than herself, who hadn't spent months blowing up like a pink balloon to bear Mark's children, who had no stretch marks on her stomach, no breasts that would never be small and firm again, who didn't have to spend hours shopping, cleaning, cooking every day, or wear the sort of clothes which didn't matter if they were spoilt when a baby was sick on them or chucked prune juice in her lap.

How serious was the affair? Was Mark going to leave her? Most of all Sancha wanted the answer to that question Mark had avoided—was he actually in love with the blonde girl?

Of course, Jacqui Farrar would have known all along about his business worries; she worked in his office—he would have been talking to her about it ever since this crisis started.

'Why didn't you tell me before?' she asked, her throat stinging with jealousy.

'When was I supposed to do that?' he bit back, his eyes dark with resentment. 'When did you ever want to talk to me, listen to me? When did you ever show any interest in my job? I'd come home and find you half-asleep over the dinner table, or you would sit yawning for a few minutes then wander off to bed.'

'You could have tried! You never gave me a hint that you had worries on your mind.' Her jealousy slipped out, her brown eyes almost black with it. 'You preferred to talk to your blonde girlfriend!'

'At least she listened to me!'

'I bet she did! While she was climbing into your bed, no doubt! Is that where you usually talk business? Is sleeping with you part of her job?'

Mark's colour came up again, a dark, angry red. He grabbed Sancha by the shoulders and shook her like a rag doll, her red-brown hair tumbling over her face, blinding her.

'You vicious little cat!'

Sancha was so mad that she kicked his ankle— kicked him so hard that she stubbed her toe and yelped with pain.

Mark yelped, too, letting go of her and stumbling back, clutching his foot.

'My God, that hurt! You could have broken my ankle!'

'Maybe next time you'll think twice about man-handling me!'

Rubbing his ankle, Mark contemplated her as if he had never seen her before, then his eyes focused on her tousled hair.

Abstractedly he muttered, 'Your hair's different... when did you have that done?'

'Oh, you finally noticed!' she retorted sarcastically. 'Days ago, as it happens—but you never gave me a second look. And you talk about feeling invisible!'

His grey eyes scanned her from head to foot, taking in the silky jade-green dress, which clung to her body from her warm, rounded breasts down over her slim waist and smooth hips, giving her a feminine shape she had not had all those months when she was disguised as sexless by her old jeans and shirts.

Frowning, he said slowly, 'The dress, too—that's new, isn't it?'

'Yes.' A wave of heat ran over her as he stared; pulses began to beat at her neck, her wrists, deep in her body.

His mouth twisted sardonically, his lids half-drawn over mocking grey eyes. 'What's the idea, Sancha?'

The rose flush in her face deepened; she looked away.

'Well, shall I guess?' Mark drawled. 'You got the letter when?'

'A couple of days ago,' she admitted, still unable to meet his eyes.

'A couple of days ago,' he repeated sardonically. 'So you rushed out and had your hair done, bought yourself new clothes, got yourself a new image... Now why did you do all that, I wonder? Don't tell me you were going to try to seduce me? Was that what you had in mind, Sancha?'

'No!' she protested at once, but she knew she was lying, because what else had she had in mind?

He knew she was lying, too, and laughed in a way that made her burn with shame and humiliation.

'Liar!'

Her nerves prickled at the deep, taunting purr of his voice. She wished she hadn't taken Zoe's advice; she had made Mark despise her, made him laugh at her.

'Come on, then,' he tormented. 'Make your pass, Sancha. You've got me here—we're alone; show me how much you still want me.'

'Stop it!' she muttered, turning away, her head bent to hide the hot flush of her face, the glitter of tears in her eyes. At that instant she almost hated him.

She had to get away from the mockery in his face. Without looking at him again, she ran out of the room, headed for the stairs, struggling with sobs. How could he talk to her, look at her like that? Did he hate her?

They had been so much in love once, in the first year of their marriage, before the children began arriving. She remembered with an agonising pang the happiness, the excitement of those days, when just to see him across a room had made her body vibrate with desire, with joy, when his grey eyes had been brilliant with an answering emotion. They had wanted nobody else then, only aching to be alone, to explore each other, bodily and mentally, discovering everything about each other, wanting to know everything about each other.

She had believed then that the arrival of the children would cement that deep bond, would bind them closer, and at first she had thought it had. It had all changed so gradually she didn't really know when the gap had begun to open between them, but, looking back, she could see now how it had widened, day by day, week by week.

Oh, Mark, how has it all gone so wrong? she thought, closing her bedroom door.

Before it had shut Mark was at the other side, pushing it open again. Sancha was afraid to make too much noise in case the children woke up. She fell back, angry, upset, alarmed, whispering, 'Leave me alone! I can't take any more. Leave me alone.'

'Not tonight, Sancha,' he said, with a sensual menace that made her blood run cold in panic and her mouth go dry with a very different emotion.

She didn't want to feel like that, not now, not while he was involved with someone else; she couldn't bear the idea of him touching her until she was sure that that affair was over.

Whatever Mark thought, she hadn't been trying to seduce him tonight. She had had a blow to her self-esteem. Finding out that your husband was having an affair with someone else could do a lot of damage to the way you felt about yourself. She had looked in the mirror and realised what a mess she was, so she had gone out to change her image as much for her own sake as to make Mark see her in a new way.

She looked at him unhappily, hating the cynical glitter in his eyes. He kept saying she was not the girl he had married—well, he wasn't the man she had married, either. Her Mark would never have treated her this way.

'Please go away, Mark. This may be your idea of a joke, but I'm not amused.'

'I wasn't trying to be amusing,' he said, taking off his tie.

Her pulses beat wildly. She retreated even further. 'You don't really think I'd sleep with you while you're having an affair with another woman?' Her voice held shock, an appalled incredulity. 'Get out of here, Mark!'

Unbuttoning his shirt, he drawled softly, 'Your bed or mine?' and real terror prickled under her skin.

'Stop it, now!' she yelled, glad that her voice didn't actually shake, although she couldn't stop trembling.

His shirt open, he sat down on the edge of his bed and began to take off his shoes. He did it so casually, it was such an ordinary, everyday thing to do. She knew it wasn't a joke then. That was when she began to believe he really meant it; he was going to force her, and she knew she would die if he did. She would never get over it.

She ran towards the door, but Mark was instantly up on his feet again, and, fleet as a panther, he loped after her, barefoot, making no sound at all. Fear spread through her veins; she was desperate to escape from him, she couldn't bear to have him touch her in this mood, but he caught her and hustled her, fighting every step of the way, back towards the bed.

Struggling, she looked up at him, tears in her eyes. 'I won't, Mark ... Get your hands off me—how can you do this? I'm not sharing you with your mistress!'

He pushed her down on the bed and came with her, the lean, powerful body falling on top of her and crushing her down, so that she couldn't get up again, couldn't escape from the sensation of that familiar, beloved weight of his body. So long. It was so long since he had lain on top of her like this.

A quiver of arousal ran through her; she couldn't stop it. She wanted him. She couldn't pretend to herself that she didn't and she didn't know if she could pretend to him.

But she must; she must stop him. If she let this hot, aching desire for him carry her away she would lose her self-respect. He was doing this to hurt her, humiliate her—she knew he was angry with her, he had told her so just now. If Mark made love to her in this mood it would only be as a punishment.

She must not let him get to her.

She averted her face and tightened every muscle in her body in angry resistance.

'Leave me alone, Mark!'

Catching her face between his hands, Mark pulled her head round towards him again, tilted her head backwards so that she couldn't pull away. For a moment they stared at each other, Sancha's eyes wide and dark with defiance and anger, Mark's unreadable, the glitter of the irises shielding the thoughts behind them.

She opened her mouth to tell him what she thought of him, but before she could get a word out his mouth was on hers in a fierce, insistent demand that made every pulse in her body wake.

How long? she thought, unable to stop her lips from moving hungrily underneath his. How long since he kissed me?

Why had she ever forgotten this drowning pleasure? How could she have been such a fool as to let anything come between them? Why hadn't she realised she was losing him?

She had been frozen, numb, for months after Flora's birth; she hadn't wanted to be touched, to make love, she had trudged on, day after day, just about making it from morning till night, keeping her eyes fixed on what she had to do, on the necessary tasks of a mother and housewife—because even to look up was to risk being unable to go on—forgetting Mark, having no attention left for him, no time, no energy and certainly no instinct of desire.

Now the ice was shattering. His hands wandered down from her face, his fingertips brushed her breasts and she groaned. Her body was emerging from the ice that had held it captive for so long; she burned with passion and desire. But she couldn't let him make love to her tonight. She mustn't surrender now, while he was still sleeping with someone else. The affair had to end first.

She had to stop him. Now. Before it was too late, before her stupid body betrayed her. Every inch of her skin was so hot; she was on fire, and deep inside her she ached with need, was almost mindless with the longing to have him buried in her, feel him moving on top of her, driving them both to frenzy.

But she couldn't. Wouldn't let him. Not while he was betraying her.

Wrenching her head away, she pushed angrily at his shoulders, trying to dislodge him.

'No! I won't let you, Mark!' she yelled loudly, far too loudly, forgetting the sleeping children, and next door Flora woke up and began to whimper.

Sancha stiffened, listening. Flora's whimper grew louder, turned into a wail.

'Mummee... Mummee... Mummee...'

She sounded so small and helpless. Sancha knew that noise—Flora had had one of her bad dreams, the dreams she could never describe or explain. Anything could bring one on...a fairy story, something she saw on television, even something she saw in the garden. Flora was full of energy and spirit most of the time, but she was terrified of insects. Moths, spiders, wasps, caterpillars... all sent her into hysterics. Her brothers thought it was funny to creep up on her and drop a spider or a furry caterpillar on her dress—they would roar with laughter as Flora flailed her arms about, screaming.

'She'll wake the others; I must go to her,' Sancha said. 'Let me up, Mark.'

His voice was harsh and angry. 'Ignore her for once! You've spoilt that child. She knows she only has to yell loudly enough to get her own way.'

'I can't—you know I can't... I must go to her...' She pushed at his shoulders harder, and with a rough, wordless snarl of rage Mark rolled to one side. Sancha slid off the bed and ran out of the room.

Flora was sitting up in her cot, moonlight on her flushed and tearstained face. She held out her arms.

'Mummee...'

Sancha picked her up and sat down with her on a chair, rocking her small, warm body; Flora put her thumb in her mouth and sighed, safe at last, her body slackening.

Sancha didn't ask her any questions about the bad dream; it would only keep Flora wakeful, stop her relaxing. She began to sing a slow, comforting lullaby under her breath, and felt the child's body grow heavier as sleep crept up on her again. Five minutes later Sancha slid her back into her cot, covered her lightly and crept out.

Her bedroom was empty, the lights on; there was no sign of Mark. Sancha stood by the door, looking around, noticing that the clothes he had taken off had gone, too—had he decided to sleep in the spare room again? Or had he gone back downstairs?

Biting her lower lip, Sancha tried to decide what to do—after what had just happened between them maybe she should wait to talk to him until tomorrow morning?

If she followed him into the spare room he would probably take it as another invitation, would try to make love to her again.

But if she didn't follow him he might leave before she got up tomorrow, and she must talk to him. Mark had tried to distract her by making love to her, but he wasn't winning at that game. They had to talk about his affair. She needed to know.

She half turned to go in search of him, then froze as she heard the sound of his car coming out of the garage.

Sancha ran to the window to look out and saw his tail-lights disappearing down the drive.

Misery overwhelmed her. Where was he going? But she knew, of course. Well, where else could he be going? To *her*, his mistress. After trying to force his wife to sleep with him he was now going to the other woman. He was going to spend the night with her.

How could he? Sancha felt sick; she couldn't fight it down. Her hand at her mouth, she ran into her bathroom and threw up.

When she had stopped being sick she took a shower and went to bed, knowing she wouldn't sleep. Her mind wouldn't stop showing her images of Mark with the other woman in bed, his naked body moving...

Stop it, stop it, she thought. I don't want to think about it. I don't want to know. How could he, after touching me like that, after kissing me, making me feel so...?

The memory of her own helpless desire was shameful. She hated him for making her feel that way and then going off to the other woman's bed.

Maybe Zoe was right. Maybe the only thing to do now was ask him for a divorce.

CHAPTER FOUR

SANCHA slept badly again and got up very early, but the spare room was empty; there was no sign of Mark. Flora, for once, was still asleep, lying on her front with her bottom stuck up in the air. Sancha left her and went into the boys' room. When she drew the curtains golden light flooded in; with bitter irony Sancha saw that it was going to be a beautiful day. To match her mood it should have been grey and rainy this morning—but then there would have been no hope of the children going out for the day with Martha, and Sancha needed some time alone.

She turned from the lovely morning to find the boys slowly waking up, yawning, reluctantly stretching under their duvets. Charlie's eyes snapped open suddenly and he sat up almost in the same instant, his hair tousled and his face pink with sleep.

'The zoo! What time is it, Mummy? Is it time to go? Is Auntie Martha here? Wake up, Felix—we're going to the zoo!'

Sliding out of bed, he rushed off to the bathroom to get there first. It was a daily battle between him and his older brother. They both fought to be first in the bathroom, first at the breakfast table, first into the car with their father. First at everything. They were in permanent competition. They might still be tiny, but they were very male, and in an earlier society they would have had all the instincts necessary to succeed in life.

Felix woke up, sat up, jumped out almost in one movement, and began capering about, chanting, 'We're going to the zoo, zoo, zoo... I'm a kangaroo-roo-roo...'

'Shh...' Sancha hissed, laying out their clothes for the day: underwear, socks, jeans and tartan shirts, and light summer sweaters in case the day turned cold later. 'You'll wake your sister.'

She was too late. From her room Flora began yelling. 'Up. Mummee...up! Want to get up!' The springs of her cot were creaking already as she started jumping up and down.

The next half-hour was as chaotic as mornings usually were; Sancha did as she always did, put her head down and got on with things without letting herself think about anything else. The boys were so excited that they didn't finish their breakfast, but nothing stopped Flora eating; she sat in her highchair happily pushing cereal into her mouth and trying to eat her banana at the same time. Sancha didn't look; it made life easier.

Martha arrived just as Sancha was clearing the table. Bright-eyed and looking almost as excited as the children, she watched Sancha putting them into their anoraks.

'Now, you be good for Auntie Martha,' Sancha told them, and the boys looked scornful.

'Of course we will, Mum!'

Flora nodded vehemently. 'Good,' she promised. 'Good for Auntie Marty.'

Sancha brought out Flora's pushchair; she would never be able to walk far, although she loved getting about under her own steam. Martha put it into the back of her car, along with a box of colouring pencils and three exercise books to keep the children quiet at the zoo when they, or Martha, got tired of running around.

Sancha kissed both boys and helped them clamber into the car, clicked home their seat belts, then put Flora's little car seat into the back, popped her into it and did up her seat belt. Flora caught her in a strangling hug.

'Bye-bye, Mummee... Bye-bye...'

Sancha hugged her back, half reluctant to let go of that warm, cuddly body. However tiring Flora was, she was the breath of Sancha's life.

'Have a lovely time, all of you,' Sancha said, closing the door on them.

Flora let out a roar, her eyes bright with sudden tears. 'Effelunt, effelunt... want my effelunt.'

Flora groaned and rushed back indoors to find the toy on the kitchen floor, where Flora had dropped it.

Flora received it with a beam and hugged it to her. Sancha shut the car door once more, and turned to grimace at Martha.

'Are you sure you can manage the three of them?'

'Of course I can! You just forget they exist until I bring them back tonight.'

Sighing, Sancha said, 'Thanks, you're a life-saver. I don't know how to thank you enough—it's so good of you to do this. If they're naughty bring them home. Don't feel you have to keep them out all day.'

'Don't worry about me—or us! I'm going to have a wonderful day,' Martha said, looking so bright-eyed that Sancha had to believe her. 'I love your kids. I've always enjoyed looking after them.'

'You're crazy, but thanks a million times,' Sancha said, and Martha got behind the wheel, waving.

The car drove away a moment later, and Sancha stood waving until they were all out of sight before going back into the house to have a leisurely bath—something she could rarely do. Normally she only had time for a hurried shower in the morning. Leaving Flora alone was always fraught with danger. You never knew what she would think of doing next, often with disastrous consequences.

The house seemed oddly quiet and empty. Sancha took ages over her bath, soaking in warm, scented water, lying back with closed eyes, her body limp and soothed. She tried not to think about Mark—that would shatter any restful mood in an instant. Instead, she emptied her mind, almost lulled to sleep by the warmth and freedom.

Eventually the water started to cool, so she got out and towelled herself dry before getting dressed in a skirt she rarely wore—pale dove-grey, pleated, it would have been ruined by any contact with Flora. It had been expensive four years ago, when she'd bought it for a family wedding, and still looked very elegant—even if her waist seemed to have expanded a little since she'd last worn it, so that she only just managed to do up the zip.

Having babies was not good for your figure. She didn't eat much, and ran around after the children all day, so she had not put on any significant weight, but somehow she was no longer the same shape as she had been when she'd first got married.

At twenty she had been tiny and slender, almost boyish, with high, small, firm breasts. After three children her breasts had filled out, were now round and soft from breastfeeding, and her hips were more rounded, too, her waist that inch or so wider. She was certainly no longer boyish in shape, although since Flora was born she had lost a lot of weight just rushing about all day. But her body had lost the elasticity which would have helped it spring back into shape.

At least the terracotta silk shirt which clung to her breasts gave her face a glow and added lustre to her red-brown hair. The soft material felt good on her skin, too, made her feel more feminine.

Downstairs in the kitchen, she looked at her watch and saw with shock that it was gone ten. Where was Mark?

But she could guess where he was, couldn't she? She stood by the phone, her hand outstretched—should she ring the blonde girl's number and ask for Mark?

No, she couldn't bear to humiliate herself like that. It would be some sort of admission—a confession that she expected Mark to be with the other girl. Sancha wasn't going to do that; she was not going to give either of them the satisfaction.

Maybe she should drive round to that apartment block in Alamo Street... what had the letter said it was called? The Crown Tower? She remembered it as the name came back to her—it was a well-known local landmark; people had talked a lot about it when it first went up. It was a modern, purpose-built block with battlements on the roof which made it look a little like a crown—although which came first, the design or the name, Sancha had no idea.

Sancha could drive there now, to check if Mark's car was parked in the car park below the tower. A shiver ran down her spine. But what if he looked out of the window and saw her? That would be even more humiliating. She couldn't bear the thought of him watching her from the other girl's flat, of Jacqui Farrar staring down at her, too. They might laugh at her together.

But they were probably still in bed. Mark had always enjoyed lying in bed for hours at weekends. Making slow, sensual, passionate love. It had been the best time of the week for them before the children came.

Her stomach heaved, her eyes closed; her jaw ached with tension and pain. How could he? Oh, how could he? Until now she had never been jealous—she wasn't the jealous type. She had never been consumed with suspicion or spent time brooding about Mark and other women. Now jealousy sat on her shoulders like a vulture, the claws tearing at her night and day.

To keep herself occupied and stop herself thinking about Mark, she tidied the rooms downstairs. She had already made the beds and tidied upstairs. At ten-thirty she made herself some strong black coffee and sat down in the kitchen to drink it.

She was going to have to come to some decision—but her mind was in such turmoil that she couldn't keep any idea in her head for longer than a few minutes. She changed all the time—she loved Mark, she hated Mark; she was going to divorce him and take everything she could get, she couldn't bear to lose him and would fight to the death to keep him. Her feelings were like a stormy sea, throwing her first this way and then that.

She did not hear the car. The first she knew of Mark's return was the sound of his key in the front door.

Instantly, her heart flipped like a landed fish, and she suddenly could not breathe. It reminded her of how she had felt when they'd first met and she'd fallen in love. She had been unable to meet his eyes, so shy she stammered if she spoke, yet so happy the air had seemed to glisten with rainbows every time Mark was near her. But that had been a magical time, and nothing was magical any more.

Listening to his footsteps crossing the hall, she stared at her coffee, fighting to look calm even if she didn't feel like that. The kitchen door opened and she felt him there, across the room, staring at her averted profile.

Angry words boiled on her tongue, but she didn't trust herself to say anything in case she burst into tears.

The silence seemed to drag on and on. At last Mark spoke, in a deep, harsh voice which made her nerves jump.

'We need to talk. Where are the children?'

She took a deep breath and managed to answer in a voice that sounded quite calm. 'Martha's taken them out for the day. To the zoo.'

He smiled sarcastically. 'How convenient. Was that your idea or hers? I suppose you've been confiding in her? Telling her what a rat I am? I don't like that, Sancha, I don't want you talking to the neighbours about me. I suppose you've talked to that sister of yours, too? I can guess what she had to say—she's never liked me much, has she?'

He walked over towards her, every move he made vibrating with anger, and she lost her head. Jumping up, she backed away too quickly, skidded on the tiled floor she had mopped not long ago and lost her balance.

Mark shot forward and caught her before she hit the floor. As his arm went round her Sancha felt her heart constrict; all the blood in it seemed to rush out and her head swam.

'Don't!' she muttered, her knees giving so that his arm tightened, to hold her up. She was reacting like a schoolgirl; she couldn't believe she was making such a fool of herself. For heaven's sake, how stupid could you get?

This man was her husband! They had three children, had been married for years—was she crazy, feeling like this just because he'd put an arm round her and held her?

'You aren't going to faint, are you? Have you eaten this morning?' Mark muttered, looking down at her, their faces so close she could feel the warmth of his skin, hear his breathing.

She was so conscious of him that her heartbeat nearly deafened her. Somehow she whispered, 'I'm not hungry. I had orange juice with the kids, and coffee.'

'How can you be so stupid?' he exploded. 'Where's your common sense? Would you let one of the kids go without breakfast?' His voice was harsh, grated with anger. He couldn't be that angry over her not eating breakfast; something else was making him furious—and she could guess what it was; she knew Mark.

If he was planning to leave her, the last thing he'd want was to feel guilty about her. He wouldn't want to feel concern for her; he would resent needing to think about her at all.

'I'm fine,' she said stubbornly, not looking at him, her lids lowered to hide the pain in her eyes. She wasn't betraying herself to him.

'You're not fine! You're looking ill. Your skin's so pale . . .' He brushed her cheek with one index finger and the touch of his skin on hers again brought a rush of colour to her face, her lashes stirring against her hot cheek.

Mark's brows lifted steeply; he watched her, then said drily, 'Well, you were. Now you're very flushed.'

Hurriedly, appalled by her own inability to control her feelings, she pulled away from him with some force, and his arm dropped.

'Would you like some coffee?' Sancha asked, to cover the awkwardness of the moment.

'Please,' he said shortly, and sat down while she got it for him. While she moved about she was very aware of him watching her, his cool grey eyes wandering from her new hairstyle to observe the way her silk top clung to her breasts, the swirl of her pale grey pleated skirt.

She put the coffee in front of him and he lifted his eyes to stare at her face.

'Is that outfit new too? What is this? Have you been on a shopping spree? How much is all this costing me?'

'I've had these clothes for four years!' Didn't he even notice what she wore any more? How could he forget seeing her in this skirt? She remembered the first time she'd worn it, at that wedding, remembered Mark telling her how much he liked it.

His voice grated again. 'Then why haven't you worn them, instead of those everlasting jeans?'

'Jeans are practical,' she told him doggedly. 'Especially in winter—they're warmer than skirts and if they get dirty you can just chuck them in the washing machine. This skirt is so pale it shows every little mark, and it costs a fortune to have to keep sending it to the cleaner's every time I wear it.'

They were talking about anything but the subject on their minds, and they both knew it. It was ridiculous how hard it was for them to talk now—that was another symptom of the breakdown of their marriage. There was this great, blank abyss between them; it made Sancha dizzy to look down into it and see the depth and breadth of the gap that had opened up.

'Well, it looks good on you,' Mark drawled, his grey eyes gleaming like pale water behind his black lashes. 'I'd forgotten what great legs you have.'

She felt herself blushing. Did he mean it? Or was he trying to distract her, bamboozle her with compliments? The trouble was, she wanted to believe he meant it, but how did she dare? She had to get herself under control and use her brains, not let her senses and her heart get the better of her.

'Don't think I've forgotten that you didn't come home last night!' she muttered, her jealousy making her voice shake. 'Where were you all night? As if I can't guess! You've been with *her*, haven't you? Oh, don't lie about it; it's obvious. You've spent the night with her, yet you think you can walk in here—'

'I didn't,' he interrupted tersely, his curt voice making her start.

They stared at each other. She saw a little tic beating beside his mouth. Mark was very angry; that tic only showed at times of strain—when he was under pressure, worried, upset.

He took a deep breath and went on quietly, 'I didn't spend the night with Jacqui, or anyone else. Last night I stayed at the motel just outside town. I drove straight over there when I left here, and took one of their chalets. Check on it if you want to! Ring them and ask—or drive out there yourself and quiz the maids. There were two single beds; I occupied only one of them—and believe me it was scarcely wide enough for me. There wasn't room for two people to share it!'

She believed him; the hard, grey stare of those eyes told her he was telling the truth. A little sigh of relief rose to her lips.

Mark heard it and frowned again, then said, in the same brusque, angry voice, 'We can't go on like this, Sancha.'

Fear made her stomach plunge sickeningly. Was he going to ask her for a divorce?

Only last night she had decided she was going to divorce him, yet now she was terrified that that was what he wanted. Why couldn't she make up her mind and stick to a decision? Why did she keep changing her mind?

What mind? she thought bitterly. She had no mind; she was just a fool. A fool whose emotions were in total flux, changing every other minute.

She looked up again and found Mark watching her with that black-browed frown, his mouth a white line, his face hard.

Fiercely, Sancha broke out, 'What decisions do we have to make, Mark? About us? Before we get to that I'd like to hear the truth about you and Jacqui Farrar. Are you having an affair with her or not? And how long has it been going on?'

He got up and walked across the room with a fierce, loping prowl. His back to her, he muttered, 'Nothing's been "going on", as you put it. I haven't had an affair with her.'

Her first sharp relief gave way to angry doubt as he added, 'Not exactly.'

'Not exactly?' she repeated. 'What does that mean?'

'It all depends what you mean by an affair. I haven't been sleeping with her, if that's what you mean.'

She wanted so badly to believe him that she had to bite down on her lip to stop herself giving a little sob. When she felt able to speak without bursting into tears, she asked huskily, 'What do *you* mean—that's the point! If you haven't been sleeping with her, what has been going on? I know something has, Mark, it's obvious from the way you reacted when I showed you that letter. It was obvious you were guilty of something. A blind man could see that.'

Mark made a noise like a groan. 'You see, we...I mean, I... She's so... Oh, God, it's so hard to put it into words.'

'Try telling the truth!' she told him angrily. 'All you have to do is tell me the truth, Mark. That shouldn't be hard.'

'It is, though. We're not talking about facts here— we're talking about feelings, and those aren't so easy to pin down.'

'Your feelings or hers?' Sancha asked, watching him with jealous, hurt eyes. Was he admitting he was in love with the blonde girl?

'Both,' he confessed, not looking at her.

She drew a long, harsh breath. 'OK,' she said a moment later, sounding surprisingly calm to her own ears, and, she hoped, to his. 'Let's start with yours. Are you in love with her?'

He was a long time answering, and as the seconds ticked by Sancha's body pulsed with a worsening pain. He was going to say yes. He was going to admit it. She knew he was and she couldn't bear to hear him say the words.

Mark sighed then. 'I think I could be.'

Could be? Did that mean he wasn't, yet?

'I think I almost am,' he added huskily, and her stomach sank again. Did that mean he was, after all, but didn't like to say so too openly?

He was playing with her like a cat with a mouse; every word he said was like having claws dug into her.

Hoarsely she broke out, 'Stop talking in riddles, Mark! Either you are or you aren't. For God's sake, which is it?'

His grey eyes darkening, he said, 'I told you, it isn't easy to talk about feelings! It all happened so gradually. I was under terrible pressure at work; I needed someone to talk to. You never had time to take any notice of me—but Jacqui did. She listened to my worries; she was supportive and sympathetic— very kind to me. She's a nice girl!'

And in love with you? thought Sancha. She must be. Every word Mark said made that much clear. Jacqui Farrar wasn't just a good assistant, ready to be there for him whenever he needed a sympathetic ear. Their relationship had gone beyond a business one. The anonymous letter-writer must have picked up something, or why would he or she have written that letter? Jacqui's feelings must be easy to read, even if Mark denied it. Maybe she had even talked about how she felt to friends? Perhaps dropped hints that Mark felt the same way?

'But we've never been to bed together,' Mark added flatly.

She watched him intently. His eyes met hers: level, steady, very serious—was he telling the truth? Yes. She was convinced by that gaze; Mark was not lying.

A deep, thankful relief filled her, but then he said offhandedly, 'Although we almost did, once.'

The admission made her stiffen, her colour going again.

Mark saw the look on her face and said fiercely, 'Well, what can you expect? We haven't made love for months. *Months*, Sancha! I'm human, after all. I'm not cut out for a monk's life, even if you are.'

Her mind was going crazy with images of them kissing, touching each other, maybe lying on a bed together, undressing each other—the pictures were being burnt into her brain; she knew she would never forget them.

'What stopped you?' she asked harshly.

He gave her a fierce stare. 'I suppose I wasn't ready to walk away from my marriage yet. I wanted to make love to her; I admit it. I almost did. But I stopped at the last minute. Somehow I just...' He took a long breath. 'Just couldn't.'

Guilt? she wondered unhappily. Or hadn't he been sure how he felt about Jacqui Farrar? He had said he hadn't been ready to walk away from their marriage yet—did he still feel something for her? She was afraid to hope—yet—but a little flame flickered somewhere inside her.

In a low, husky voice she asked him, 'What about her? How did she take you changing your mind?'

Mark's frown etched deep into his temples. 'I won't talk about Jacqui's feelings, Sancha. Only about my own. I told you, she's a nice girl. Don't blame her. All this is down to me.'

Giving him a derisive look, Sancha said, 'It can't be, Mark. It takes two. If you nearly slept with her then she must have been encouraging you. Don't tell me she isn't in love with you, because she must be— or she wouldn't have let you get that far.'

He looked away uneasily. 'It isn't fair on her to talk about her to you, Sancha. How would you feel, in her place?'

'I wouldn't let myself get involved with a married man! Let alone one with three small children!'

Jacqui Farrar must have been working hard for a long time to lure him into her flat, into her bed—how had she felt when Mark had backed off at the last moment? Had she been furious?

'How...how long ago was this?' she whispered.

'Oh, for heaven's sake, Sancha, I've told you the whole truth—can we stop this inquest now? What good will it do to go into all the details?'

'I need to know! Was it recent, this time when you almost slept with her?'

He was angrily flushed now. 'Yes,' he bit out. 'If you have to know. It was the other night.'

She froze. 'The day the anonymous letter came? The day you lied to me and said you were having dinner with your boss, but were actually at Jacqui Farrar's flat?'

Mark looked at her sharply. 'What are you getting at? You think Jacqui sent that letter? Of course she didn't!'

'Didn't she? I wonder. Think about it, Mark! She meant to get you into bed; she wanted me to come to her flat that evening and catch you both.'

Sancha didn't buy this image of the blonde girl as sweet and kind and absolutely innocent. Men were such fools about women; they didn't understand the way their minds worked. Mark was clever, and he was very shrewd in dealing with other men, but he was blind where women were concerned. He simply didn't see past the pretty surface.

'Jacqui wouldn't do a thing like that! She isn't the calculating sort. Neither of us got into this relationship deliberately. We both just drifted into it—it just happened!'

He might believe that. Sancha didn't. Someone had once said that there was no such thing as an accident; everything that happened had a root cause.

She didn't entirely blame Jacqui Farrar. After talking to Mark, she had to admit that she, herself, was partly to blame for his straying; she had put her marriage on hold two years ago, giving her children all her attention, almost forgetting Mark existed. He had become part of the furniture.

But Jacqui Farrar had taken advantage of the situation. She had homed in on Mark's loneliness and unhappiness and realised he was wide open to any woman who paid him attention. Mark wasn't the type to flirt with other women; that was not what he needed. He needed to feel loved, cared about, listened to—he should have got all that from her, Sancha, not had to go to someone else to find it.

'Can we leave Jacqui out of it?' he said again, impatiently.

Sancha shook her head. 'How can we? While she works with you every day you're going to be seeing her all the time, and you can bet she isn't going to let go—so how can we leave her out of it?'

His grey eyes darkened, and he said sharply, 'The problem isn't Jacqui—it's you and me, Sancha. Our marriage is on the rocks—what are we going to do about it?'

She swallowed, trembling. 'What do you want to do about it?' And then she waited, her heart in her throat, for him to ask her for a divorce. If he did, she would refuse—point-blank. She wasn't letting him go; he belonged to her.

He looked at her explosively, as if he wanted to hit her. 'Are you leaving it to me? Does that mean it doesn't matter to you? That you don't give a damn if I go or stay?'

Fear made her just as angry. 'Don't put words in my mouth! I asked you what you wanted to do. Don't try and turn it round to make it my decision. It was a straight question—just give me a straight answer!'

'Don't shout at me, Sancha!' he said, his face alive with rage. 'You keep blaming Jacqui, but if I almost strayed it was your fault, not hers, because you've been shutting me out ever since Flora was born. And now you're throwing all the responsibility for our marriage on me, when it's just as much up to you what happens next. You asked me what I wanted to do—well, I'm asking you. What do *you* want to happen? I can't go on like this—it's a nightmare. Make up your mind. Do you want a divorce?'

CHAPTER FIVE

THE question made her whole body shake. Bending her head, she whispered, 'No, of course I don't!' Did he really believe she wanted their marriage to end? If Mark thought she wanted a divorce the gap between them was even wider than she had imagined. He couldn't know her at all.

But then how well did she know him? She hadn't suspected he was involved with someone else, had she? The shock of that discovery was still reverberating inside her head. He hadn't told her about his problems at work, either, or made her realise that he was so angry with her because he felt she no longer cared about him. How had she missed that? What else about Mark didn't she know?

In fact, did she really know Mark at all? And how well did Mark know her?

They had been married all this time, but they seemed to be strangers; during the past couple of years they had grown apart without her noticing it. And Sancha found that so confusing and disturbing she couldn't think straight.

Mark suddenly moved, and she jumped to find him very close. Putting one long index finger under her chin, he pushed her head up so that she had to look at him, her brown eyes wide, dark, unhappy between long, curling lashes.

She didn't want this stranger who was her husband
to look so searchingly at her, to see too much of the
pain and longing and bewilderment she felt.

'Don't,' she said, trying to pull free, and he
frowned. His stare dropped to her trembling mouth.

'Don't what, Sancha?' he ground out between his
teeth. 'Don't what? Don't touch you? Come near you?
You've been telling me that for too long; I'm sick of
being told to keep my hands off you ...'

'I never said that!'

'Oh, not in words, no. But in so many other ways—
your whole body said it every time I was anywhere
near you. It's saying it now.'

'No, Mark! You're imagining it!'

'Am I?'

He ran his finger upwards to stroke along her mouth
and she quivered, wanting to pull away but fighting
it. He would take that as proof of his accusations,
and maybe that was what it was, this nervous uncertainty, this fear of being so close to him, of being
touched by him. When had it started, this reluctance
to be near him?

She loved him, and she wanted him, yet she did not
want him to touch her. He was right.

'You've misunderstood,' she said confusedly.

Mark's sardonic smile made her flush. 'OK, tell me
you want me to touch you, Sancha!'

She couldn't make a sound, torn between wanting
him intensely, nervously dreading it, and hating the
thought that he was taunting her, mocking her. Only
the other night Mark had almost gone to bed with
another woman. Sancha did not want him until she
could be sure he was hers—entirely and completely

hers. She didn't want him back if his heart was elsewhere.

She needed time to relax with him, time to get to know him again, this familiar stranger who had once been her lover and was now a man she wasn't even sure she knew at all.

'No answer?' he muttered, holding her eyes as if trying to read the mind behind them.

She looked away, butterflies of panic fluttering in her stomach. 'You're making me nervous...' She took a breath, went on, 'You're making me shy, self-conscious...' Sancha wanted to explain how she felt, make him see that she no longer felt she knew him, but the words wouldn't come out.

'Shy?' he said softly, and slowly moved his other hand. She jerked in shock as his fingers lightly touched her breast, moving intimately against the silk shirt, caressing the contour of her flesh, following the rounded fullness down into the deep valley between.

'I'm not ready to... You said... Mark, we have to talk...' Her body was shifting restlessly as his thumb stroked her nipple, making her flesh grow hot and aching under the caress.

'Talk, then,' he said in a deep, husky voice. 'Tell me how this feels...' He leant forward and his mouth brushed her throat, slowly moving downwards to her shoulderbone, then pushing aside her shirt to travel along the smooth skin into the warmth between her breasts.

Sancha gave a stifled groan of protest and pleasure, pulling away, fighting her own desire, resisting his, but Mark's arm went round her, holding her so that she couldn't get away. His head nuzzled at her insistently, pushing her back over his arm, so far back that she almost lost her balance. He undid the buttons on her shirt, pulled aside her bra and the lacy white slip she wore, his lips hotly exploring the naked flesh he had uncovered.

The sensation was so intense it was painful. She clutched at him, her head swimming, her eyes closing as if she was fainting, but that wasn't what was happening—she wasn't fainting; she was drowning, sinking under the temptation of his hands and mouth. He was touching her with all the sensuality and fire that had always been between them in the beginning.

Why had she let herself lose this miracle of feeling? What had happened to her to make her forget how it could feel to be in his arms, given up to this seduction of the senses?

Mark's mouth slid upwards to her throat again, and then it was on her lips, coaxing them apart, his tongue sliding inside. Sancha kissed him back, her body so weak with pleasure she couldn't stand, only Mark's arm around her keeping her upright.

Holding her tightly, Mark lowered her to the floor. Lost to everything but the flame beating higher and higher inside her, Sancha didn't realise what was happening until she felt the tiled floor touch her back.

The tiles were cold; the shock of the contact on her hot flesh was like the shock of having cold water thrown in your face on a hot day. She gave a gasp, her eyes flying wide open, and looked up to see Mark's face an inch or two away from her, his body just lowering itself onto hers.

'No!' she burst out, shuddering, and rolled sideways to escape him. She was on her feet before Mark could react.

He lay there, for a second or two, on his face. She could hear him breathing raggedly. Then he got up, too, darkly flushed, his eyes glittering as he stared at her.

'Sancha, for God's sake, don't stop now... You want it, I want it, we both need it—you know we do!' He held out his hands; they were trembling slightly. 'See that? That's how much I want you.'

'As much as you wanted *her* the other night?' she asked bitterly and he shut his eyes, groaning, turning away.

'Oh, not again! Do we have to bring that up again? Forget Jacqui!'

'I can't. Can you? Working with her every day, seeing her, being alone with her? You may not have slept with her—but you admit you almost did. Is she going to accept the end of the affair...?'

'We never had an affair! We saw each other for a little while. OK. I admit that. But it was not an affair. We had a few dates, that's all.'

'That's all?' She was so angry she was shaking. 'What went on between you on those dates, Mark? You kissed? Held hands? Touched each other?'

He stared at her, face shuttered, eyes hooded, mouth a tight white line. He didn't deny it; his very silence was an admission.

'And you don't call it an affair?' Sancha muttered hoarsely, jealousy clawing at her.

'We never slept together!'

'Is that all you think love is? Sleeping together?' How typical of a man, how blinkered and blind to the realities of life. Sancha looked at him impatiently. 'Mark, you must have had feelings about her! And she must have feelings towards you!'

He sat down at the table and bent his head, staring at his empty coffee-cup. Sancha watched him, automatically doing up the buttons of her shirt with fingers that trembled.

'I'll talk to her, explain,' he said after a long moment.

'Well, tell her this—she can't go on working for you, Mark! It wouldn't be fair to her, or to me. She would always be a threat to our marriage.'

'I can't sack her! That wouldn't be fair—you must see that! I suppose I can ask her if she'll agree to work for someone else.'

'If she is still in the building you'll be seeing her all the time!'

'I'll talk to her,' he said again, doggedly. He stood up. 'She may prefer to get another job, but I cannot sack her, Sancha.' He looked at his watch. 'I suppose I'd better deal with it right away. You obviously aren't going to be satisfied until I've told her it's over.'

Sancha felt a stab of terror. She didn't believe the other woman was going to let him go easily. Jacqui Farrar would fight to keep him; Sancha was sure of it. She knew she would herself, in the other woman's place. Jacqui Farrar would try to seduce him. And Mark was so frustrated and aroused at this moment that he was going to be vulnerable to temptation.

Why, oh, why had she been such a fool that she had let their marriage drift so close to the rocks?

'We'll both go,' she said impulsively, and Mark did a double take, his grey eyes fierce.

'You're not serious! What are you trying to do to me? It will look as if you've given me an ultimatum and you're coming along to make sure I do what I'm told.' Angry red burnt along his upper cheekbones.

'I'd be humiliated. Are you trying to destroy my self-respect? Is that what you want, Sancha?'

She flushed, too, hurt. 'Of course not! I'm just afraid of what will happen if you see her alone.'

'You'll have to trust me.' His grey eyes stared into hers. 'Or *don't* you trust me, Sancha?'

'It isn't you I don't trust—it's her! If she's in love with you she isn't just going to stand there and listen; she'll argue, try to make you change your mind.'

'You don't know her or you wouldn't say things like that about her! Jacqui isn't some predatory, clinging female, she's a—'

'Nice girl!' Sancha finished furiously. 'I know. You said. But I don't think you know much about women, Mark. I think this "nice girl" is going to fight like blue blazes to hang onto you.'

Mark shook his head, frowning. 'I'd never have believed you could be this cynical, Sancha. You don't know her. I do. I've treated Jacqui badly—I should never have started seeing her out of work.'

'No, you shouldn't!' snapped Sancha, angry about being called cynical. 'And if I am cynical, who was it taught me to be that way?'

'If we're getting into that old argument about what came first, the chicken or the egg,' Mark snarled, 'I'll say again what I said before . . . If I even looked elsewhere it was because you no longer seemed interested.'

She bit her lip. 'It wasn't true, though, Mark. I was just so tired. What with a difficult pregnancy, and then Flora being such a demanding baby, I simply had no energy for making love any more. I didn't realise how you were feeling; I was just too busy trying to cope.'

He sighed, nodding. 'I know. Look, can we have a pact, Sancha? Let's stop quarrelling and blaming each other, forget all this ancient history and start again?'

'We can't so long as Jacqui Farrar is still in your life, Mark! You must see that.' She paused. 'I have to know... Who made the first move—you or her?' She needed to know that which showed how little she really knew him—why didn't she know the answer already?

He looked impatiently at her. 'Nobody made a move. We just had dinner one night after work because we'd been working so late; that's how it began. It wasn't a date the first time, it was just two colleagues eating together. But slowly the atmosphere changed between us, things got personal, and then we started being secretive, furtive... lying to people at work—and I lied to you about having to work late. We were in the middle of a relationship before we realised it. And I blame myself more than her.'

Sancha laughed shortly. 'Well, I blame her more than you—she knew you were married, with three children!'

'So did I, for God's sake! I had no business letting anything happen between us. That's why—Sancha, try to understand this—I have to see her myself, alone. I simply can't go there handcuffed to you as if I can't be trusted to talk to her without you there to tell me what to say!'

He walked towards the door and Sancha followed him, agitation beating inside her like the wings of a dying bird.

'Mark, don't go to her home! Don't be alone with her. Wait till Monday and see her at the office.' The other girl couldn't try to seduce him there.

He turned to glare at her. 'I can't afford to have any scenes at the office! You must see that! Look, I won't be long. I'll be back as soon as I can. Why don't we go out to lunch for once, as we don't have to take the kids with us? We haven't been to The Oak House in a long time—ring and book a table for one o'clock. I'll be back in time to drive us there.'

The front door slammed behind him and she stood there, frozen on the spot, listening to his car driving away, staring at the clock and registering that it was eleven-thirty now. He had been here an hour; the time had flown. Now he had gone again, and she knew the time would drag like a corpse until he was back.

She walked over to the phone and rang their favourite restaurant, The Oak House, an old Georgian pub on the outskirts of town, to book a table for one o'clock. Mark was right; they hadn't been there for so long she couldn't remember the last time, and didn't recognise the voice of the man who answered.

'That isn't Jules, is it?' Sancha said uncertainly, nevertheless picking up his French accent.

'I'm afraid Jules left six months ago,' the voice said, in good but strongly accented English. 'I am the new manager, Pierre.'

'Oh, hello, I'm ringing to book a table for two for lunch at one today.'

'A moment, please ... hmmm ... yes, we do have a table for you. Can I take your name, please?'

'Crofton—Mrs Crofton.'

There was a brief pause then he said with a smile in his voice, 'But of course, Mrs Crofton—we are always delighted to see you and your husband. I will give you the same table you had last week.'

Sancha put down the phone in a numb silence. She knew, of course, what it meant—Mark had been taking Jacqui Farrar to *their* restaurant!

That was bad enough. But they had been booking in as Mr and Mrs Crofton. The waiters would all know at once that Sancha was not the woman who had been going there as Mark's wife all this time. The new manager had been there six months. Had Mark and that other woman been going there as husband and wife all those months?

Sancha knew she couldn't walk in there with Mark now, with those waiters staring at her, whispering, gossiping behind her back. And she couldn't ring back and cancel—Mark would have to do it.

Her nerves were scraped so raw that when the doorbell jangled she almost jumped out of her skin, and it was a minute or two before she pulled herself together enough to go to the front door.

Zoe was on the doorstep, looking even more glamorous than usual in skintight white jeans and a vivid emerald-green silk shirt over which she wore a black suede waistcoat which clipped her waist as tightly as a belt.

She gave her sister a searching look. 'Hey, are you OK?' Her eyes narrowed. 'What's happened? You look like death warmed up. Talked to Mark?'

'Yes, we've talked.'

Zoe did not miss the harshness of her voice. 'Hmm,' she murmured, probing Sancha's face mercilessly. 'Do I gather the news isn't good? Come on, you might as well tell me—you know you will in the end! What's going on, Sancha?'

She peered over her sister's shoulder. 'Kids about? That's really why we came—Guy asked if I'd like to go to a fair he'd heard about, over at Ramsden, and it occurred to me that it might help you if we took the kids with us. Guy's still a kid at heart, himself. He'll take care of them on the rides, don't worry, and we can stop and have fish and chips on the way, so you won't have to make lunch for them. You can spend the afternoon with Mark and talk properly.'

Sancha managed a wavering smile. 'Thanks, you're very thoughtful, Zoe, but actually Martha has taken them out for the day, to the zoo.'

Zoe's brows lifted. 'Nice of her. Was that your idea or hers?'

'Hers.'

'But you had told her? About Mark, I mean?'

'Martha's a good friend.' Sancha stared past her sister at the red Porsche parked at the kerb. The driver was watching them through the open window of the car, his head turned their way, the warm spring breeze blowing his hair about. 'Is that Guy in the Porsche?'

'Yes, that's Guy, our producer.' Zoe grinned. 'I have to be nice to him to make sure we get enough money.'

'You know you fancy him—even I know that!' They had talked about him often enough for Sancha to pick that much up, although Zoe was always cagey about her private life—or perhaps reluctant to take it too seriously herself. For Zoe, her career came first, but Guy had been around for quite a long time now and Sancha knew she saw a lot of him.

He wasn't good-looking—a big, craggy man with a lot of tousled brown hair and broad shoulders—but there was something reassuring about his face: a calmness, a humour that Sancha liked. He would need that to cope with Zoe.

Behind her the phone suddenly began to ring, and Sancha hurriedly ran to pick it up.

'Hello?' she said breathlessly.

A muffled, indistinct voice said quickly, 'Your husband is with her now, at her flat, if you want to catch them in bed together. Or don't you care?'

'Who is this?' Sancha asked hoarsely, but the only reply was the sound of the phone slamming down.

Sancha hung up, too, shaking with rage. She turned and found Zoe had followed her into the house and was right behind her now. Zoe looked at her intently, frowning.

'Who was that?'

'It was her...I'm certain it was her... She'd disguised her voice—she was talking through a handkerchief, or something, and I didn't recognise the voice—but I'm sure it was her.'

Zoe didn't need to ask who she meant. 'What did she say to you to make you look like that?' Her vivid green eyes skated over her sister's ashen face, and Sancha turned her head to escape that clear-sighted stare.

'She said Mark was at her flat, if I wanted to catch them in bed together.'

'What a b—' Zoe stopped, frowned again, looking angry. '*Is* he? He isn't here, I take it?'

Sancha shook her head. 'He went to see her ten minutes ago.' She saw Zoe's expression and quickly added, 'Oh, he told me he was going—to tell her it was over. I've told him she has to stop working for him, that he can't go on seeing her, either in the office or out of it, if he wants to stay married.'

Zoe's lip curled sardonically. 'Well, if that's what you want, I'm happy for you, but in my experience when a man strays he usually gets the habit. But don't let me talk you out of taking Mark back.'

She took a pen and a small notepad out of her black suede shoulder-bag, picked up the phone and began to dial.

'What are you doing? You're not ringing her?' Horrified, Sancha tried to take the phone away from her, but Zoe blocked her with one arm, holding her away, the receiver clamped to her ear.

After a minute, without speaking, she scribbled something on her notepad, then, still silent, hung up. Sancha watched her in bewilderment.

Turning to Sancha, Zoe held out the pad. 'Is that her number?'

Sancha had difficulty reading it; the figures seemed to dance up and down like black flies on the white paper. When she managed to focus properly, though, she recognised the number at once. She knew she wouldn't forget it for a long time.

'Yes, that's it. Did she answer?' she whispered. 'What were you trying to prove?'

'Having children seems to turn the brain to marshmallow,' Zoe told her sarcastically. 'Haven't you heard that you can now trace the last call by dialling this number?' She wrote the number down, holding the pad out again. 'When you dial that number you're told where your last call came from! Unless the person who made that call dials another number first, to block you—which really makes nonsense of the whole thing if you're trying to catch a phone pervert. But they say that everyone has the right to privacy, even if it means that sick guys can still make scary calls to women without being traced.'

Sancha was barely listening. 'So it *was* her ringing me! And she must have sent that letter, too,' she thought aloud.

'Oh, obviously.' Zoe nodded. 'It's a dirty tricks campaign, darling.'

Sancha looked at her blankly. 'What?'

'She's trying to get you worked up enough to kick Mark out and ask for a divorce. Nice lady. What are you going to do?'

'Tell Mark,' Sancha said fiercely. 'Maybe that will make him realise she isn't the sweet innocent he seems to think she is!'

'Men are as blind as moles where women are concerned, Sancha. It's odd how easy it is for some women to fool them, and yet they're so tricky themselves.' Zoe shot her a sharp look. 'Does Mark admit he has been having an affair?'

'He says it hasn't got serious.'

'What does that mean?'

'They haven't actually—' Sancha broke off, then wailed, 'I don't want to talk about it, Zoe!'

Zoe wouldn't be put off. 'They haven't slept together? Did you believe him?'

'Yes!' Sancha snapped.

Zoe smiled at her suddenly. 'Then why do you sound so defiant?'

Somebody knocked on the front door; they both looked round, eyes startled. Guy stood outside, smiling at them both in a lazy, laid-back way.

'Hi, what's going on, then? Are we taking the kids to the fair or not?' His voice was warm and deep, a very pleasant sound which made him instantly likeable.

'Apparently they're already having a day out, at the zoo,' said Zoe, smiling at him in a way that told Sancha just how much she liked him, for all her cynicism about men.

'Oh, well, just us for the big dipper, then,' he drawled with a teasing little smile. 'And then I can seduce you in the Ghost Train when the skeletons come rattling out of the dark, making you scream and throw yourself at me.'

'Fat chance,' said Zoe. 'It will probably be you who gets scared stiff and throw yourself at me—and I'll throw you right back.'

'Can I give you two some coffee?' Sancha offered with automatic courtesy, feeling sorry for Guy, whose rueful expression was rather sweet. Zoe was always slapping him down, keeping him at bay; how long would he go on pursuing a woman who treated him like a stray dog she found appealing now and then, but wasn't sure she wanted around permanently?

It was Zoe, of course, who made the decision. 'No, thanks, we ought to be on our way to the fair. Come on, Guy.'

He followed like an obedient dog, padding along beside her, his long, graceful body supple. Zoe paused at the front door and looked at her sister drily. 'Be firm with Mark, Sancha. Don't let him get away with anything. But I'm beginning to think he isn't lying, or why is she so desperate to convince you otherwise?'

When they had driven away Sancha stood at the kitchen window staring out into the sunlit garden, brooding. What was happening over at Jacqui Farrar's flat? Was Zoe right? Was the blonde girl trying too hard to convince her of Mark's guilt?

Oh, she wished she could be a fly on the wall in that flat. She needed to know the truth. She wanted to trust Mark, to believe him, but jealousy kept blinding her like dust thrown in her eyes.

The time kept ticking by... She looked at her watch and saw it was a quarter past twelve. Where was Mark? Was he coming back or not?

She paced to and fro, listening to the weight of silence in the house. It was so long since she had been alone like this, without the children, with no chatter or running feet, no childish voices breaking in on her thoughts. It was a strange, disturbing experience. She could hear all the little sounds of the house as she normally never did because the children's noisiness drowned them out. The tick, tick, tick of the clock in the hall, the faint whisper of the water heating, the hum of the washing machine in which she had some clothes soaking, the little creak of the wooden flooring as the sun warmed it. The house was alive, a living being, with her inside it.

Oh, where was Mark? A look at her watch told her it was now twenty past twelve—only five minutes had dragged past.

It had felt like hours. She paced some more, listened to the sounds of the house some more, watched a bird fly past the window, then heard a car driving past and stiffened, but it did not stop. It was not Mark.

She looked at the clock and it was nearly half past twelve now. He had said he would be back by now.

He wasn't coming. He was with that woman. In that flat. In her bed.

Sancha put a hand over her mouth to stop herself screaming.

CHAPTER SIX

AT ONE o'clock she started putting together a salad for her lunch, although the last thing she wanted to do was eat. She just needed something to do, something to keep her hands busy and her mind empty.

Wasn't it ironic? Ever since she'd had her first baby she had spent her days in hectic activity, now and then wishing she had time for herself, time to have a life of her own apart from the kids and the housework. Now, today, she had the whole day to herself—and she hated it.

At twenty past one the phone rang; she stood there like a dumbstruck fool, staring at it, not wanting to answer it in case it was Mark telling her he wasn't coming home—he had chosen Jacqui Farrar after all and wanted a divorce.

The ringing went on and on, and suddenly she thought, He might have had an accident! He was upset, he drove away from here in such a state... What if he had crashed?

She ran to pick up the phone, her skin icy cold and dewed with the sweat of fear.

'Hello?' she said in a breathy, hardly audible voice.

'Mrs Crofton? This is The Oak House.' The voice was not friendly, and she couldn't blame him.

'Oh,' was all she could manage for a second.

'You had a booking for lunch at one o'clock,' the manager said coldly. 'We have been holding the table but we have a long queue of people wanting to eat here, so if you are going to be much later we shall regretfully have to cancel your booking.'

'Yes, of course,' she said stupidly. 'I'm sorry, my husband seems to have been delayed. He said he would be back nearly an hour ago, but he hasn't arrived. I'm sorry.'

Her husky, stammered explanation did not improve the manager's mood. Icily he said, 'Very well, Mrs Crofton. I would have appreciated it if you could have let me know earlier. I have turned people away who could have occupied that table.'

'I'm sorry,' she said again, and the phone went down with a bang.

She sighed, replacing her own. That was one restaurant they would never be visiting again. For several reasons. She never wanted to go there now she knew that Mark had taken Jacqui Farrar there, and the restaurant manager would probably never take a booking from them again anyway.

She looked at her watch and saw that it was now almost half past one. Mark would soon have been gone for two hours. It didn't take that long to say goodbye to someone.

When Jacqui Farrar rang here, thought Sancha, Mark must have just driven up to the block of flats. She must have seen him from her window and immediately rung with that lie about him being in bed with her. What had she hoped to achieve? Had she hoped to bring Sancha hurrying over there to catch them together?

So she must have set the scene, to make her story convincing. Feverishly, Sancha began working out what must have happened.

The blonde girl might have got up late—maybe she had just got out of bed, had still been in her night-dress? Or, more likely, by that time of day on a Saturday she had been up for some time, had had a shower, was dressed. She would have dashed into her bedroom, taken off her clothes and put on something seductive and alluring—a sexy nightie with a matching negligee—so that when Mark rang her doorbell she could spray herself from head to foot with some musky, inviting perfume, run a dishevelling hand through her hair and go to let him in looking as if she had just got up.

No doubt Mark would immediately have started trying to tell her it was all over, and that was when she would have begun to cry. And when he tried to comfort her he would have found her coiling around him like bindweed.

Sancha had had bindweed in the garden last year; it had been very pretty, with great pink and white trumpets flowering on curling green stems, but it had grown like lightning, strangling other plants in its path, and had tried to take over the whole place. It was ruthless, determined to take over everywhere; you had to be just as ruthless back.

She had got rid of it in the end—chopping roots, pulling the stuff up, root and branch, burning it on the garden bonfire. She would have to be just as merciless with Jacqui Farrar.

If it wasn't too late. Why had she let him go to that girl's flat? She had known, hadn't she, that it was dangerous? Jacqui Farrar obviously had no scruples; she wouldn't just let him go, give up gracefully.

And neither will I! Sancha thought, her teeth tight. I'm not giving up, either. He's my husband, I love him, and I'm going to fight for him. I can fight just as hard as she can, too! I've invested years of my life in Mark; he's the father of my children and I'm not standing back and watching him walk away with another woman. What sort of woman is she, trying to take my husband away from me? How can she live with herself?

But it takes two, doesn't it?

Mark wasn't some toy she and Jacqui Farrar were fighting over. He was a grown man with a mind of his own and a very strong will. Why had he ever got involved with another woman in the first place? Because he hadn't been getting whatever he needed from her, obviously. She sighed, closing her eyes. It would be so easy to blame Mark or this other woman for what had happened—but nothing in this world was ever that easy. She had to accept that she took some of the blame too.

Oh, she could give any number of reasons for their slow drift apart over the last couple of years—it was always easy to make excuses for yourself. But marriage, like every other part of life, was something you had to work at, something you had to keep in constant good repair. Both of you. That was where they had failed.

She and Mark had stopped giving each other the love and support they each needed; their marriage had begun to die slowly over the months when they'd been too busy with other things to care about each other. If she had encouraged Mark to talk about his problems, had listened, been more loving, he wouldn't have gone elsewhere for sympathy. If Mark had only noticed how tired she was, had tried to help, had been more understanding, had offered her tenderness . . .

If, if, if. They had missed so many opportunities. They mustn't miss any more!

The familiar note of his car's engine made her stiffen. She ran to look out of the window and saw Mark driving into the garage. Relief hit her in a tidal wave; she closed her eyes briefly, light-headed, dizzy, then pulled herself together. She hurried back into the kitchen and began to finish the preparations for their lunch. With the salad she would serve a choice of cold sliced chicken—the remains of a roast she had cooked a couple of days ago—or grilled goat's cheese on crisply toasted French bread. She turned on the grill, began to slice the creamy cheese.

While she was doing that Mark walked into the kitchen. Sancha put down the knife she was using and turned to face him, wiping her hands on some kitchen towel. What was he going to tell her? That he had changed his mind? That it was their marriage that was over, not his affair with the blonde girl?

Mark looked grim, as if he had had a shock. 'I'm sorry I'm late,' he said curtly. 'What about lunch at The Oak House? Did you manage to book?'

'Yes, for one o'clock. They rang back at half past one and cancelled, and they weren't very happy.' She met his eyes deliberately. 'I gather you ate there last week. With your wife.'

He closed his eyes. What was he hiding? Was he afraid she would read something in his eyes? Or didn't he want to see her? 'Oh, God,' he groaned. 'Did she book us in as...?'

'Mr and Mrs Crofton. Yes. The manager naturally assumed I was her, and reminded me that I often ate there with my husband,' Sancha said in a voice she managed to hold level. She wasn't going to let this degenerate into a nasty scene; they had had enough of those already. Somehow she would hang onto her cool, let Mark dictate the way this went.

His eyes opened again, their grey dark with anger. 'Not often, Sancha! It was only once—last week. It was her birthday. She said she wanted to go somewhere special, and she knew The Oak House was my favourite restaurant—I'd mentioned that—so she asked if we could eat there and I said fine. And she made the booking.'

'For Mr and Mrs Crofton!' Despite her good intentions, Sancha's voice rose. 'Don't tell me you didn't realise they thought she was your wife?'

Mark raked a hand through his hair in a gesture of frustrated rage. 'I remember they did say something about hoping my wife had enjoyed her meal. I should have corrected them, but at the time it didn't seem important. I would have felt embarrassed, saying, No, this is my assistant, not my wife. I didn't realise she had deliberately lied to them.'

'She lies a lot,' said Sancha, and Mark gave her a quick, sharp look.

'What does that mean?'

'She rang me, not long after you had gone...'

'Rang you?' He looked disturbed, as well he might.

'She tried to disguise her voice, but it was her, all right. I'm certain of it.' Sancha watched him, trying to read his expression, wishing she knew if he had been lying to her all along. 'She told me you were at her flat in bed with her.'

Mark's face tightened as if she had hit him, his skin flushing an angry red. Slowly he said, 'You're sure it was her? You recognised her voice?'

'I thought I did at the time—and then Zoe rang some number which tells you where your last call came from, and it was Jacqui Farrar's number. So then I knew for sure.'

His frown deepened, etching lines across his forehead. 'Zoe? What was Zoe doing here?'

'She and her producer dropped in to offer to take the kids out for the day. She was still here, talking to me, when the call came.'

'And you told her all about it!' Mark's voice was hard with fury; Sancha felt as if he had slapped her.

'I was upset; she could see that. She's my sister and she cares about me—why shouldn't I confide in her? I had to talk to someone.' She was fighting with tears now, and Mark might have been able to hear that in her voice.

He looked at her uncertainly, sighing. 'All the same, I wish you hadn't. I don't want the world and his wife knowing all about our private life.'

'Zoe isn't the world and his wife; she's my sister! She knows me, and she could see how much the phone call upset me!'

His voice gentler, Mark said, 'I'm sorry if you were upset, Sancha—but for God's sake, you must have known what Jacqui said on the phone was a lie. I wouldn't have gone to bed with her. You knew I had gone there to tell her it was all over.'

Her lower lip trembled; she bit down on the inside of it to stop the trembling and whispered, 'How was I to be sure? I didn't know what to think. You might have lied to me. You might have changed your mind once you saw her. I didn't know if I could trust you. I'd had the ground cut from under my feet by that letter and I didn't have the self-confidence to be sure what to believe any more.'

'Is that really how you feel?' Mark said slowly, frowning. 'I'm sorry, Sancha, I know what you must have been through—I've been through it myself, all these months, when I thought you no longer loved me. We're going to have to start trusting each other again. It won't be easy, I know that—but you can believe this, I swear. I've fired her.'

Sancha inhaled sharply, searching his face for signs of how he felt. There was darkness in the grey eyes, a hard compression at his mouth; she knew the signs. Mark was angry—but with whom? With herself for demanding that he sack Jacqui Farrar? With himself for giving in? Had it been a hard decision to make? Had he been in love with the blonde girl after all?

Jealousy bit into her. 'What happened when you told her?'

His mouth twisted with distaste. 'There was a very unpleasant scene. Look, I don't want to talk about it, Sancha. Can we forget her now? She is out of my life.'

Sancha looked down at the kitchen table, struggling with pain and uncertainty. Seeing the food she had been preparing, she automatically turned to the practical routines of her married life for comfort and reassurance.

What else did she have to hold on to while everything in her life kept dissolving underneath her? At the moment she felt as if she had no solid ground to stand on, as if the earth kept quaking under her feet.

'I've made a salad—what would you like with it? Shall I grill this goat's cheese, or would you just like some of the cold chicken left over from the other day?'

He made a tired gesture. 'Whatever you like. I'm not hungry.'

At once she was concerned, studying the tense, weary outline of his face and seeing the lines of strain in it. Mark didn't look well, and that was unusual— he was normally a powerful, active, healthy man.

'You ought to eat,' she murmured anxiously. 'It will make you feel better; it always does. You need the blood sugar.'

'I need a drink,' Mark said, walking away into the sitting-room.

She heard him pulling the cork out of a bottle of wine, pouring himself a drink, and sighed, pushing the goat's cheese and slices of French bread under the grill.

How were they ever to get back to normal? Life would never be the same again. The tension between them made her jaws ache and her face felt tight and icy. Was that how Mark felt? Probably; it was certainly how he looked.

She snatched the cheese from under the grill before it burnt, then walked to the door of the sitting-room. 'Do you mind if we eat in the kitchen? It will be easier.'

Mark turned, a glass of white wine in his hand, and looked at her from some frozen distance, his eyes remote. He nodded. 'Fine, whatever you like. Shall I bring the wine and a glass for you?'

'Please,' she said, not caring whether she had a glass of wine or not, but thinking that wine might help the atmosphere between them. They both needed to relax, to unwind.

They sat down and Mark poured her wine, moved the glass over next to her plate, then looked at the grilled goat's cheese, the crust golden and crisp, the interior soft and melting, on the lightly toasted bread.

'This looks good. We first ate it in Normandy, do you remember? At the *auberge* just outside Bayeaux?'

He was making conversation, small talk, as if they were strangers. And that was what they were, wasn't it? The time since Flora was born had pulled them far apart; they had each changed during those two years. They were different people now, and they would have to get to know each other all over again.

'I remember,' she said, shivering a little because the memory was of hot sunshine, laughter, happiness, a time when they had still been passionate lovers, a time when family life hadn't swallowed up their youth. And today she felt chilled and sad.

Eating some of the cheese, Mark said, 'This really is good—was it marinated in olive oil before you cooked it?'

'No, but I sprinkled a little olive oil on it before I put it under the grill.'

'It's terrific,' Mark said, finishing his wine.

'Thank you, I'm glad you enjoyed it,' she said, smiling with pleasure. When you had spent time preparing a meal it was good to know it was appreciated. So often in the past he had eaten her food without seeming to notice what she'd put in front of him.

He poured himself another glass of wine, sipped it, then said abruptly, 'By the way, I've been thinking... I wonder if she sent you that anonymous letter.'

'I'm sure she did.' She looked up and their eyes met; Mark grimaced.

'She really took me in, you know. I never suspected what she was really like. She put on a very convincing performance. She seemed such a nice girl. But when

I told her we had to stop seeing each other the mask came off. She threw herself at me, clung to me like a limpet.' He looked away, his face harsh. 'She even tried to get me into bed.'

Sancha listened, unsurprised—wasn't that exactly what she had pictured would happen when he told the other woman it was over?

Mark said flatly, 'And when that failed she turned very nasty; she tried to threaten me with lawyers— said she was going to sue me and she was going to sell her story to the newspapers!'

Startled, Sancha asked anxiously, 'Do you think she will?'

Mark's strongly moulded face tightened and his grey eyes flashed. 'I don't give a damn what she does— and I doubt if any newspaper would be in the least interested. After all, I'm not some film star, or anybody famous—and neither is she! Why should anybody want to read about us? She was just trying to throw a scare into me.'

'I knew she wouldn't let you go easily,' Sancha whispered, her hand clenching on the table.

Mark took hold of it between both of his, their warmth and strength enclosing her cold, trembling fingers. 'Don't look so scared,' he soothed. 'She can't hurt you, darling. I won't let her.'

He hadn't called her darling for a long, long time. She gave him a wavering smile, her eyes wide and brilliant, and Mark smiled back.

'Come on, now, eat your lunch before this cheese goes cold! The salad is really delicious too. I love the dressing—what is it?'

'Just a French dressing—some of the raspberry vinegar I brought back from France last autumn added to olive oil with a little mustard and honey.'

'It makes all the difference to the salad. We couldn't have eaten better anywhere else. I'm glad we stayed at home.'

'So am I. We couldn't have talked properly in a restaurant.' Or been so honest with each other, she thought. 'Mark, how do you really think this shareholders' meeting is going to go? Do you think you and Frank can get them to see that selling to Grainger could be a mistake?'

He lifted his shoulders in a wry shrug. 'We'll do our damnedest, but I wouldn't bet on it. Grainger's offer is tempting, his shares are more than twice as valuable as ours and the deal he's offering them is a very good one—looked at in a strictly neutral fashion, I have to admit that. I wish I could deny it.'

Hotly, Sancha said, 'But you and Frank have done so much to build up the company! Surely they'll realise that? You've both worked so hard, and they've just sat back and raked in their profit—if they sell you out now it will be so unfair!'

He smiled at her. 'I couldn't agree more, but shareholders only think about one thing—how much money they can make out of a company. They don't even stop to think about the consequences for everyone who works for it—the selling off of assets, all the job losses.'

'Will many people lose their jobs, then?' she asked anxiously.

'Highly likely. In take-over situations, there are usually job losses—starting at the top and going right on down the firm.'

'If it comes to it ... if ... what will you do, Mark?'

His face was grim, his mouth pale and tense. 'No idea, yet—but ... we might have to sell this house and get a smaller one, I'm afraid. And we might have to move away from here, if I get a job with another firm.'

That was a shock, and she could see in his eyes that he was worried about her reaction to this news, but so long as they were together nothing else mattered. She lifted her chin and gave him a reassuring smile. 'Well, we've lived in smaller houses before. We'll manage.'

She saw the relief fill his face. 'You won't mind?'

She grinned at him. 'It could even be fun—like starting again!'

'It might be, at that,' he agreed eagerly, then asked, 'What time will Martha be bringing the kids back?'

'She said late afternoon.'

'That gives us plenty of time to ...' He looked at her through his black lashes, his mouth curving in a faintly teasing smile. 'Talk,' he finished softly, with deliberate ambiguity.

Sancha felt her pulses begin to race. Talk was not what he had in mind, his mocking eyes made that clear, and although she had told him firmly that she would not let him make love to her until she felt sure she could trust him again, she knew how vulnerable she was to him, and was afraid Mark had guessed, too. She didn't seem able to hide her response whenever he came near her.

She brought out a bowl of fresh fruit when they had finished their meal, but Mark said he didn't want anything else to eat—the salad had been perfect, now he just wanted coffee.

'I'll bring it into the sitting-room. Go and sit down. I won't be a minute,' Sancha said, but Mark shook his head.

'I'll help. It's ages since I did, I always used to—remember?'

She remembered well. It seemed so long ago, those first years of their marriage, when even the dull routine of tidying up and washing dishes had been fun if they did it together.

He cleared the table and loaded the dishwasher while she was making the coffee and laying a tray, then he carried the tray through to the sitting-room for her.

Sancha sat down on the floor beside their low coffee-table and poured two cups of black coffee; Mark put a tape of soft music on the music centre and then walked over towards her, every step he took sending shock waves through her. She was so intensely aware of being alone with him that she couldn't look at him.

Hurriedly she held out his coffee. Mark gave her a wry twist of a smile, his eyes telling her that he knew why she was so flushed, why her hand shook as she gave him the cup.

She quickly got to her feet with her own coffee and sank into an armchair. It seemed perfectly natural, she hoped, but it was a sort of flight—she was inwardly running away as hard as she could. Mark's expression told her she wasn't fooling him for an instant. He didn't comment, though. He took the chair opposite her, his long legs stretched out casually, his body folding back into the deep comfort of the seat.

The silence lingered; Mark's eyes were half closed, slumberous, as if he was already half asleep after their meal, yet something in his hooded gaze made the hair on the back of her neck prickle. What was he thinking? Sancha was so nervous she had to say something to fill the vacuum, distract him from whatever was on his mind.

'I hope the kids aren't too much of a handful for Martha. She has often had them for a few hours, but she isn't used to coping with them for a whole day.'

'Oh, I'm sure she'll manage. She seems a very capable woman to me,' Mark drawled, then drank some of his coffee, still watching her over the brim of the cup in a way that made her intensely aware of him.

'It has been a lovely day so far,' Sancha said huskily.

'So it has,' Mark drily agreed.

'And the kids love going to the zoo.'

He laughed. 'Maybe the zoo might even like to keep one or two of them? Flora, for instance? She seems to be under the impression she's a kangaroo—I'm sure they could find room for her.'

She gave him an uncertain look—sometimes she felt he was hostile to Flora, not as fond of her as he was of the two boys.

But he grinned at her, so she knew it was just a joke, and relaxed a little.

'They grow up so fast. In a couple of years Flora will go to school and I won't have anything to do all day.' For a second or two the idea was faintly depressing.

'If you're suggesting we have another baby, forget it,' Mark said, raising his dark brows incredulously. 'What you need is a break from looking after small children, surely?'

She groaned. 'Oh, yes, I seem to have done nothing else for years! I would like some of my life back, time for myself.' Her eyes brightened. 'I might do an advanced photography course and start work again, part-time. That would be fun.'

'Why not? You were a good photographer—a pity to waste all that talent. You've spent enough of your life looking after other people, time to think about what you need.'

'And if I was earning, too, it would help our budget. That could be useful, couldn't it?'

Mark gave her a surprised but thoughtful look. 'That's true. I hadn't thought of you going back to work, but I must say the extra money would be very useful—if Grainger does get the company and I have to look for another job.'

She felt a glow of pleasure at the thought of it. Mark looked much happier now; the lines of strain and anxiety had faded from his face. She got up and went to kneel down beside the coffee-table. 'More coffee?'

Mark got up with his coffee-cup in his hand and put it on the coffee-table, but as Sancha reached for it Mark knelt beside her and reached for her. He moved faster than she did. Sancha hadn't been expecting his move and was caught off balance, one hand outstretched.

She had known he would make some sort of pass, and had made up her mind to react calmly and coolly, stay in control of the situation—but the instant he touched her she felt her whole body go crazy. She was jangling from head to foot like a mad alarm clock.

His hands linked behind her back and propelled her towards him. He smiled into her wide, startled brown eyes. 'Stop looking like a petrified rabbit hypnotised by a snake every time I come near you! Relax, Sancha. It's OK. In case you've forgotten, we are married. It isn't immoral for a husband to kiss his own wife!'

He brushed his mouth over hers; it was such a light, brief kiss it left her frustrated. She wanted more. Her mouth clung to his but he lifted his head to look into her eyes. 'See? That didn't hurt, did it?'

She wasn't so sure about that. Pain wasn't as simple as she had once thought; being kissed by a man you weren't sure of could be very painful. Pleasure held more pain than she'd ever suspected, too.

'Don't look at me like that,' Mark said sharply, and kissed her eyelids, so that she had to close them. His tongue-tip gently brushed her lashes, sending waves of pleasure through her. The tiny caress had an extreme effect on her heartbeat, sending it instantly into overdrive. Her head swam and she felt dizzy, as if she were flying, weightless, helpless.

The next time she opened her eyes she found herself lying on her back on the carpet. With a cry of dismay she looked up into Mark's grey eyes. He was arched over her, his face inches away.

'Oh! Mark . . . no . . .'

'Oh, Sancha, yes,' he mocked, leaning down closer, and the closer he came the harder her heart beat, the faster her pulses ran.

Dry-mouthed, she whispered, 'Please . . .'

'Please what, Sancha?' he asked softly. 'Please kiss you? I was going to, don't worry.'

His mouth descended as he said the last word; she didn't have time to evade it, or struggle, and as soon as it had closed over her lips she was lost. She no longer wanted to escape; she wanted to give in to the intensity of pleasure his kiss made her feel.

She closed her eyes herself that time, deliberately shutting out the world and all her anxieties and uncertainties. Why was she fighting him? Why resist what she wanted so badly? Her mouth quivered and parted under the hot pressure of his kiss; her blood began to sing in her ears. She could hear nothing, see nothing, and she gave herself up to pleasure.

Her arms ran round his neck, pulling him closer; she slid her fingers into his thick, dark hair, felt the shape of his skull under her caress, held his head between her palms. Mark groaned, undoing her silk shirt, his fingers sliding inside, his palms cupping the warm swell of her breast.

His touch made the heat between them grow like a furnace. She could hear him breathing raggedly, heard her own unsteady breathing. His hands slid up under her skirt, higher and higher, and a deep, aching need beat inside her.

She feverishly undid his shirt and kissed his rough, warm chest, hearing wild bells ringing in her ears.

Mark swore.

Sancha opened her eyes dazedly. 'What ...?'

That was when she realised the bells were not just ringing in her ears. The jangling sound filled the whole house.

Somebody was ringing the front doorbell.

'Take no notice,' Mark muttered, but a second later Sancha heard voices. Familiar, much loved voices. Calling her.

'Mummee ... where are you? Mummee ...'

'Oh, God, they're back,' Mark ground out between his teeth. 'I thought Martha promised to keep them out all day?'

Sancha hurriedly began dressing again, her fingers shaking as she slid buttons back into buttonholes, pulled down her skirt, ran her hand over her tousled hair. By then one of the children was tapping on the window of the sitting room. She knew they wouldn't be able to see her and Mark on the floor, but when she stood up she would come into their angle of vision, so she must be fully dressed before she stood up.

Mark began doing up his shirt, his mouth wry. 'Whose idea was it to have children anyway?' he asked her as she scrambled to her feet.

'Yours,' Sancha threw at him as she walked away towards the front door.

Mark groaned. 'I must have been crazy.'

When Sancha opened the front door Martha gave her a rueful, apologetic smile. 'We had a little accident,' she confessed. 'We had to come back early, I'm afraid.'

She was carrying Flora wrapped in a car rug. For a brief, terrible second Sancha's heart missed a beat in terror, then she saw that Flora was not hurt. No, Flora was beatific, beaming at her mother and leaning forward eagerly to wind her arms around Sancha's neck.

Sancha took her from Martha and discovered what sort of accident Flora had had. Under the car rug, Flora was naked. Her lovely red hair was dripping wet and tangled.

'I felled in a pond,' Flora gleefully informed her.

'I'm sorry,' said Martha, watching. 'I only took my eye off her for a minute—I was buying them an ice-cream. I heard the splash as she fell in . . . luckily it was very shallow. I fished her out almost as soon as she went in, but her clothes were drenched. I had to take them all off.'

'I got nothing on,' Flora said with a prim expression. 'Auntie Marty took all my clothes off.'

The boys were in the house, stampeding into the kitchen; Sancha could hear Mark talking to them and their excited voices answering.

'A bath for you, young lady,' she told Flora. 'Come in and have some tea, Martha.'

'No, I think I'd better get home and have a bath myself. I got my feet wet, too,' Martha said. 'I'm squelching in my shoes.'

Sancha laughed. 'Oh, I'm sorry—she's very naughty. Thank you for putting up with them for a whole day! It was very good of you.'

'I enjoyed it—even the unexpected paddle,' Martha assured her.

'Say thank you to Auntie Martha,' Sancha told Flora.

'Thank you,' Flora said, leaning forward to kiss Martha suddenly on her nose.

Martha kissed her back. 'Goodbye, sweetheart.' Then she smiled at Sancha. 'I can see the rest did you good. You've got far more colour now.'

Sancha blushed harder. Martha laughed and walked away towards her own home, and Sancha carried her squirming, naked daughter upstairs to have a bath.

Later, angelic in her favourite pyjamas, covered with teddy bears and little red hearts, Flora sat in her highchair eating scrambled egg and little fingers of toast while the boys, who had had baths after her, and were now in their pyjamas too, consumed platefuls of baked beans and toast, still talking excitedly about their day at the zoo.

Mark sat at the table drinking a cup of tea, asking them questions, listening to their garbled answers. They were over the moon to have him there, competing with each other for his attention.

Sancha wasn't saying much. She concentrated on seeing that they all ate their food and drank their orange juice without any of the usual mishaps. Even Flora didn't spill anything; her bib was perfectly clean when Sancha took it off before carrying her up to bed.

By seven o'clock all the children were fast asleep, exhausted by the pleasures of their day.

Sancha came back downstairs and found Mark in the sitting-room, watching football on television, his feet propped up on the coffee-table, his dark head back against his armchair, his long body totally relaxed and comfortable. She stood in the doorway for a moment, unnoticed, staring at him and feeling a sensation of pure happiness. For the first time in many months, all was right with her little world.

Then she remembered that in a few hours they, too, would be going to bed, and pulses sprang up all over her body.

Mark looked up, his eyes narrowing as he absorbed her expression. A mocking little smile curved his lips.

'I know what you're thinking,' he whispered, and she blushed.

'I was wondering what you might like for supper,' she lied.

'Liar,' he said, grinning. 'Why not some take-away, to save you having to cook again? It won't take me ten minutes to drive to the Chinese restaurant and back.'

'That would be fun! We haven't done that for ages.'

'There are a lot of things we haven't done for ages,' Mark murmured, his eyes half hooded, teasingly watching her colour come and go. 'We must make sure we do them all,' he added deliberately.

Sancha pretended not to get the implications. Casually she said, 'I fancy some sweet and sour chicken, and fried rice with egg and peas.'

Mark stretched, his arms raised over his head, his long legs and lean body gracefully sexy in the gesture. 'That's not what I fancy,' he teased. 'But OK—and I'll get some lamb and green peppers in black bean sauce. You like that, too, don't you?'

She nodded. 'Shall I make some green tea to go with it, or would you rather have wine?'

'Tea,' he decided, without hesitation, getting to his feet.

He left immediately and Sancha laid the table in the kitchen for two. She set out their Chinese bowls and chopsticks, heated three larger bowls in the oven, and put two candles in the middle of the table while she waited for the kettle to boil for the green tea. She had already scattered the black leaves of tea in the bottom of her porcelain Chinese teapot, decorated like the bowls with small blue figures and lotus flowers.

Mark was back just ten minutes later; as soon as she heard his key in the door Sancha poured the boiling water on the tea-leaves so that the fragrance of the infusing tea filled the room.

After handing her the large brown paper carrier bag of food Mark wrinkled his nose, inhaling the scent of the tea.

'Smells good.' He washed and dried his hands and sat down at the table as Sancha poured the food into the pre-heated bowls. Mark had also bought a bag of prawn crackers, a dish of mixed Chinese vegetables and some fried spring rolls.

'There's enough here for six!' she said, helping Mark to rice but leaving him to help himself to whatever else he wanted.

'It's a small banquet,' he agreed with satisfaction. 'I got hungry once I smelt the food in the restaurant. I did think of getting Peking duck, too, but I'd have had to wait longer.' He took a sip of tea, closing his eyes. 'Mmm . . . delicious.'

They didn't hurry over the meal, and when they had finished cleared the table and loaded the dishwasher together. Then Sancha sent Mark into the sitting-room while she made coffee. When she went through with it she found him glued to football again; this time the sports news was on television and he wanted to know the result of the match he had been watching earlier.

As soon as the news was over a film started, and they sat watching that for a couple of hours, but Sancha hardly noticed what happened in it; she was thinking about the night ahead. Each time she felt her heart race and heat flood her body.

At ten o'clock she got up. 'I think I'll have a bath before bedtime,' she said, not meeting Mark's eyes.

'See you soon,' he said softly, and she almost ran out of the room.

She took her time over her bath, a long, slow soak in fragrantly scented water, and took her time towelling herself dry, too. She dropped a delicate white silk and lace nightdress over her head, and over that a matching throat-to-toe robe, which foamed with lace. After brushing her damp hair she used her favourite French perfume, one Mark had chosen for her that Christmas.

He must be in their bedroom by now, she thought, opening the bathroom door, but as she walked across the landing she heard Mark's voice downstairs.

Sancha froze. Who was he talking to? Was there someone downstairs with him, or was he on the phone? She leaned over the balustrade to look down into the hall and felt her stomach turn over in shock and pain.

Mark stood just below her with a woman in his arms. A woman with blonde hair. Jacqui Farrar.

CHAPTER SEVEN

SANCHA was rooted to the spot for a few seconds, staring down at them, almost wondering if she was seeing things. Surely this was a nightmare, a bad dream. It couldn't really be happening. *That* woman couldn't be here, in *her* house, wearing just a tiny dark red silk dress—more like a slip, actually—hanging from her bare shoulders from tiny ribbon-like straps, the material skimming her body, the hem way above her knees, showing lots of thigh. Sancha took in the way the other woman's clinging arms clutched Mark's neck, her body leaning against his while she kissed him passionately.

Sancha almost pinched herself to make sure she was awake. Maybe she was fantasising this scene? She kept imagining Mark kissing this other woman, maybe that was what she was doing now.

She closed her eyes, then looked again—and they were still there, below her, in the hall. The blonde girl was sobbing now. 'Oh, Mark ... you're making me so unhappy. You can't just dump me now—not now. I don't believe you don't still love me.'

Huskily Mark said, 'Don't, Jacqui. Don't cry like that.' And his hands closed on the girl's slender waist as if to draw her even closer.

Sancha flinched; no, she wasn't imagining anything—the pain of this was far too real to be a dream, or even a nightmare.

128

The agony of facing reality made her head explode, as if a bomb had gone off inside her. She ran down the stairs in a flurry of silk and lace, almost tripping over the long skirts of her nightdress and robe, her eyes burning with unshed tears and impotent rage.

Mark heard the sound of her running feet and pushed the blonde away from him. He turned, his face flushed, with an expression of what Sancha knew had to be guilt in his eyes.

She looked at him contemptuously. 'Yes, it's me— and I've actually caught you with her this time, haven't I? Did you think I was still in my bath, or waiting for you in bed? No, you've been unlucky, Mark. I saw her in your arms. I heard the two of you.'

'We'll talk when she's gone,' Mark said curtly, but she wasn't going to let him talk her round. Not this time.

'How dare you?' she burst out, her voice shaking and hoarse. 'Right under my nose! Kissing her, in my own home!' She swallowed, only just keeping back her tears. 'Oh, how could you, Mark?'

'I wasn't kissing her!'

'I saw you!' He was still trying to lie. That made her even angrier. What a half-wit he must think her, if he hoped to make her doubt the evidence of her own eyes!

'You saw *her* kissing *me*!' he snapped, his face tense.

'I didn't see you resisting! You were holding her by the waist, pulling her closer.'

'I was trying to push her away.'

She gave an angry bark of disbelieving laughter. 'Do you think I was born yesterday? I know what I saw.'

'That's just it—you don't! You saw her with her arms round my neck, you saw her kissing me—but you did not see me kissing her back. I wasn't kissing her back, so you can't have seen it!'

'Oh, Mark, how can you say that?' the blonde girl broke in passionately, looking up at him with wounded eyes.

She was very pretty, Sancha thought, staring, taking in everything about her, and very young. Her hair wasn't naturally blonde; Sancha could see that close up. Nature had made her a brunette; here and there you could glimpse dark roots. She had a good body: slender but curvy, the breasts high and firm, the waist tiny, the legs well-shaped. She hadn't had any babies to spoil the shape of her breasts or give her stretch marks on her stomach.

There was something about her Sancha did not like, however—and it was not just her blatant chasing of Sancha's husband. Sensing she was being watched, Jacqui Farrar slid her a sideways look at that minute, and Sancha caught the gleam of malice in her blue eyes. There was an acquisitive curve to her hot red mouth, too. The first impression of youth, sweetness, innocence was fading already. This was a woman out hunting, and her prey was Sancha's husband. But she wasn't getting him. Not if Sancha could help it.

'Whatever he's told you, he lied,' the blonde girl said. 'He loves me. We've been having an affair for months.'

In a deep, angry voice, Mark muttered. 'Go back upstairs, Sancha, let me deal with this. We can talk later. Now not.'

She turned on him, her face cold. 'We'll talk now—I'm not leaving you alone with her.' Then fire broke through the ice of her manner. 'You lied to me! You told me you were never in love with her, and you told me it was all over!'

'It is,' he said curtly.

'No, it isn't,' the blonde girl denied, looking at Sancha with a hatred which was entirely mutual.

Sancha wanted to kill her. She was very angry with Mark, but she hated this woman who was trying to destroy her marriage, wreck her life, hurt her children. The other girl was young enough to find someone else—why was she so set on stealing another woman's husband?

'It is,' Mark repeated, his face set and bleak. 'I meant every word I said, Jacqui. Please believe me. It's over, completely and for ever.'

The blonde looked up at him, her lower lip trembling. 'You don't love her! If you did, you would never have started seeing me! You were bored with her—bored with being married, with your kids. You were going to leave her, divorce her!'

Had he promised her that? Sancha thought, her stomach churning with sickness.

As if she could read Sancha's expression, the other woman turned to her. 'He told me he was leaving you. He swore to me he would leave you,' she said bitterly. 'He said your marriage was over, that he hadn't slept with you for months and never would again!'

It all had such a ring of truth; Sancha didn't want to believe her, but she couldn't help it.

'You told her that?' she said in a low, shaking voice, looking at Mark with accusing eyes. 'How could you? You *did* talk to her about me—about us! You said you hadn't but you were lying.'

Mark took a sharp, angry breath. 'Keep your voice down, for God's sake, or you'll wake the children!'

'You're a bit late with your concern for them, aren't you? It apparently didn't bother you when you were thinking of leaving me, walking out on them!'

Through his teeth, Mark said, 'We can't talk here, in the hall, or they'll hear every word. Do you want that?'

'Of course I don't!' Sancha angrily walked away into the sitting-room and Mark followed her. Jacqui Farrar rushed after him, her brief skirts flaring around her thighs. She must be cold, coming out so skimpily dressed late at night, Sancha thought irrelevantly.

Mark switched on the light and stood in the middle of the room, his shoulders back, his hands jammed into his pockets, confronting her. Very quietly, he said, 'Sancha, take no notice of anything she says. If you let her, she'll have us at each other's throats. Don't let her sidetrack you into a row with me—that's what she wants. Can't you see that?'

'I just want you to admit the truth,' Jacqui said, tears coming into her eyes and rolling down her pale cheeks. 'You love me—you know you do. You don't love her, not any more—if you ever did. It's your marriage that's over and that's the truth. I know you say you can't afford to get divorced and then have to pay her huge alimony, but it is me you love, not her!'

Sancha felt as if she had just been kicked in the stomach. She looked at Mark in anguish. 'Is that what you told her? Is that why you're staying with me? Because you can't afford a divorce?'

Her mind was working overtime, adding it all up and coming to a conclusion she found very painful. It made sense. He had said the firm were having financial problems, and if this take-over went ahead Mark might soon be out of a job.

If they got divorced he would lose this house—it was the matrimonial home, and any settlement would award it to her and their children, to keep the family together. Apart from that, Mark would certainly have to pay her a large part of his income every month; divorce was an expensive business.

He ran his hand through his black hair with a furious, frustrated gesture.

'No! For heaven's sake, Sancha, she's lying. Take no notice of anything she says. You'd have to be blind not to see what she's up to! It's the old tactic—divide and rule. Don't let her get away with it.'

'Has he told you he still loves you?' the blonde girl asked Sancha. 'If he did, he's lying. He promised me that if I went to bed with him he would leave you, get a divorce and marry me. He doesn't love you, not any more. But then he did some sums, I suppose, and realised divorce would cost him too much, so he told me we had to stop seeing each other. But he said he still loved me, not you.'

Sancha thought back over everything Mark had said to her during the last couple of days and her heart sank. He had said a lot, but one thing he hadn't said. He hadn't told her he still loved her. There could be only one reason for that. He hadn't been able to lie.

Mark watched her eyes fill with pain and his frown deepened. 'That's enough!' he exploded, walking to the door. 'You're leaving. Now, Jacqui! And don't come back. Stay away from my home and my wife. It won't do you any good, any of this—I told you it's over and I meant it. I'm sorry if I hurt you. I shouldn't have started seeing you. It was all a stupid mistake, and I'm sorry, but it's over now.'

He went out, leaving the door wide open, but the blonde girl didn't follow. 'Whatever he tells you it will be a lie!' she hissed at Sancha. 'We've been lovers for months. He doesn't love you. He's only staying with you because he can't afford a divorce just now. Is that what you want? A husband who loves someone else but is staying with you just to fend off a divorce?'

Sancha wanted to put her hands over her ears, but she wasn't going to let Jacqui Farrar see how much she had hurt her. Instead she turned her back on the other woman and walked over to the hearth, staring at the silver-framed photographs which were arranged above the fireplace. They were a reflection of her life with Mark—the laughing faces of their children, holiday snaps, and herself and Mark on their wedding day, their bodies warmly leaning on each other as they posed for the photographer, smiling into the camera, looking so happy it hurt to see it now. She had been so blissfully unaware that marriage could hold pain as well as joy.

'You may keep him, but you'll always know he's mine, in his heart!' Jacqui Farrar said, and Sancha swung round furiously.

'No, he's mine! He's my husband and the father of my children. He belongs with us and you aren't getting him. You knew from the start that he was married—why did you go after him?'

'I didn't go after him! I didn't need to—we fell in love.'

Sancha gave her a scornful smile. 'No, that's a lie. You may have fooled Mark but you don't fool me. You're the type of woman who always wants what another woman has got. That's what really gives you a kick, isn't it? Stealing another woman's man. You're an emotional kleptomaniac...'

Very flushed, the other girl snarled, 'And what are you, then? Hanging on to a man you know doesn't love you... Haven't you got any self-respect?'

'I shouldn't talk about self-respect, if I were you. You're pretty enough to get a man of your own. Why did you have to chase a man you knew belonged to someone else? And don't try to kid me that it was Mark who did the chasing. I don't believe it. It's crystal-clear to me that you were after him from the minute you got that job with him. You only got somewhere because our marriage was going through a bad patch. Well, all that's over now. We're together again.'

'Until the next time he gets bored with you!' Jacqui Farrar sneered, just as Mark strode back into the room.

'I thought I told you to go?' He looked from one to the other of them, frowning as he saw Sancha's disturbed face. 'What's she been saying now?'

'I just told her the truth—that you love me, not her. You know you do, Mark!' Jacqui Farrar's face filled with appeal and she put out a hand to him, pleading with him, but Mark just shook his head, his face bleak.

'What does it take to get a message home to you? It is over, Jacqui. I'm sorry it ever started. I'm sorry if I hurt you, but you shouldn't have come here tonight, upsetting my wife—now, will you please go before I lose my temper?'

He grabbed her by the arm and began pulling her towards the door.

'Let go of me!' the blonde yelled, and Sancha flinched, afraid the children would wake up. She didn't want them to hear any of this. It might damage them for life. She and Zoe had had parents who loved each other; that love had given a warm security to their childhood. She wanted her children to have a happy childhood to look back on, too.

'Get your hands off me! Don't think you're getting rid of me this easily,' Jacqui Farrar threatened. 'I haven't finished with you yet.'

'Well, I've finished with you!' Mark told her with angry vehemence, hustling her out of the room into the hall. The front door opened, there was a brief sound of scuffling, and then the front door slammed shut. Silence followed and Sancha closed her eyes, shuddering.

The other woman had gone, but she had left behind a tangle of disturbing thoughts and feelings. Sancha couldn't like her, but she couldn't help feeling sorry for her. Jacqui Farrar might have chased Mark deliberately, might be the type who was excited by the idea of stealing a man from another woman, but she had loved Mark, that much was unquestionable—Sancha had seen the passion in her eyes, heard the pain in her voice. The other woman had been hurt, too. Mark had hurt them both.

He walked back into the room and Sancha felt him standing behind her, could almost hear the whir of his mind as he thought out what to say to her, how to soothe her.

'No more lies, Mark,' she whispered. 'I've had enough lying. I can't bear any more.'

His voice was quiet and firm. 'I haven't lied to you. I told you the exact truth. The lying was done by

Jacqui. From the way you talked to her just now I thought you had realised that. She was never going to let me go without a fight. You said that yourself, and you were right.'

'Whatever she has done, she's been hurt, too. I saw that just now! She really fell for you, Mark.'

'Oh, for heaven's sake, Sancha. Don't waste your pity on her! She came here to make trouble, and she succeeded, didn't she?'

'How can I believe you when you've hidden so much from me all these months?' Sancha turned and looked at him with bitterness.

Mark's black brows jerked together; his face was tense and hard, and so was his voice. 'I stopped hiding anything yesterday. You know everything that happened now.'

'Do I? How can I be sure of that? How do I know what really went on between you and that woman? You claim you never slept with her, but she says you did. You claim you didn't talk about me to her, but she says you did. Which of you am I to believe, Mark?'

He was pale now, his eyes underlined with dark shadow, his mouth a tight, white line.

'You've known me all these years—and you can ask that?' he bit out, his hands clenched at his sides.

She slowly shook her head. 'I'm not so sure I do know you. I'm beginning to think I never really knew you at all.'

'Funny, I was thinking the same about you!' he muttered.

Sancha was afraid she was going to burst into tears any minute, and she would hate him to see how much he was hurting her.

'I'm tired and I've had enough. I'm going to bed,' she said, walking towards the door, her face averted from him. She needed time to get over the emotional shocks of today. 'You can sleep in the spare room tonight,' she muttered over her shoulder.

'Like hell I will!' Mark broke out, his lips curled back in a snarl.

She stiffened in alarm at the tone of his voice, but wouldn't show him she was afraid of him. Lifting her head in defiance she hurried out of the room and crossed the hall towards the stairs, her long skirts rustling silkily around her bare legs.

Mark came after her silently, running, and the hair on the back of her neck stood up. She began running, too, up the stairs, but before she got to the top Mark caught up with her. His arm went round her waist, pulling her up, off the ground, her feet kicking; his other arm slid under her knees, lifting her up high, against his chest.

'Put me down, Mark, you'll drop me,' she whispered, afraid of waking the children. The house was so quiet now that Jacqui Farrar had gone, but it was a misleading quiet; the emotions between her and Mark were still charged and dangerous.

He didn't answer. Striding across the landing, he walked into their bedroom, closing the door with his foot.

'Put me down!' Sancha told him angrily, and he dropped her on her bed; she always slept in the one nearest the door so that she could get in and out of the room fast if a child called her in the night. Everything in her life seemed to have been arranged, for years, to fit in with the needs of her children—never her own needs, or Mark's. She had thought that

that was normal, natural, the only sensible arrangement.

She had been so wrong.

Her head whirling from the sudden descent, she looked up at Mark to protest and saw that he was getting undressed in a hurry, shedding his clothes in all directions—on the floor in a heap, some flung across a chair.

'You're not sleeping in here tonight!' Sancha told him, sitting up.

'Oh, yes, I am, and in that bed, too,' Mark said through his teeth, and the dangerous flash of his eyes made her pulses skip.

She had to look away because he was naked now and her mouth had gone dry. It wasn't easy to look away—she wanted to look at him very badly. The other night when she had walked into the spare room and seen him getting naked into bed she had ached to look and look, yearned to touch him, and Mark had made it clear he didn't want her. That had hurt; rejection always did hurt.

The irony was that he wouldn't reject her tonight, far from it. It was obvious what was on his mind and she had to stop him, but she knew that wasn't what she wanted to do. She wanted to touch him, caress that powerful male body, feel his warm skin under her fingertips, the roughness of dark hair curling down his chest, the flat stomach, the strong hips, the muscled thighs.

But she had to keep him at arm's length until she knew for sure what had happened between him and Jacqui Farrar, and whether or not their relationship was really over for good.

'I mean it, Mark! I'm not sleeping with you.' She hurriedly began to slide off the other side of the bed, but his hands caught her by the waist and dragged her backwards.

'Don't fight me, Sancha. I warn you, I'm not playing games tonight,' he muttered, pushing her down on the bed again and arching over her.

'Neither am I!' She looked angrily up at him, and then wished she hadn't, because that one glimpse made her whole body turn boneless. She shut her eyes, feeling as if she was sinking in a lift that was out of control. Any second now it would reach the bottom and crash, and she would be broken in pieces. What had happened to her self-respect? She was weak and trembling—having him so close had turned her into a jellyfish—and she was breathing so fast and raggedly that she knew he must hear it, and would know what it meant.

Mark slowly undid the ribbons tying her robe. 'Is this new, too?' he asked her huskily. 'I love the way the lace doesn't hide your nipples.' His head came down and his tongue probed sensuously through the lace.

Her breath caught. 'Don't!' What he was doing was far too enjoyable.

One of his hands cupped her breast, pushing it up so that her warm, bare flesh showed above the silk.

'Considering you've had three babies, your breasts are amazing,' he murmured, his mouth exploring. 'Better now than they were when we first met; they were quite tiny then. They're much sexier now. I remember watching you feeding Flora just after she was born, and envying her.'

His mouth opened softly around her nipple and Sancha inhaled sharply at the sensation of having him suck at her. She had always enjoyed breastfeeding her babies; his mouth tempted her, and she couldn't deny she was enjoying what he was doing, but she mustn't let him do this to her. Not yet.

But the pleasure was so intense that she couldn't push him away. She wanted to stroke his hair, hold him to her, give herself up to him.

Women had that fatal flaw—some deeply buried instinct weakened them when they knew they were needed, made them helpless to fight the seduction of having a man at their breast, like a baby, pleading for the comfort of their body.

'I need you,' Mark whispered, his hands sliding under her nightdress, between her thighs, sending a shudder of desire through her.

But desire wasn't enough. She wanted him to love her. Sancha tensed, half sitting up, pushing him away.

'Stop it, Mark! I haven't forgotten Jacqui Farrar. I won't let you make love to me until I know for sure what really happened between the two of you and I'm certain it's over for good.'

'I told you . . .'

'Yes, but that was before I saw her in your arms!'

'She threw herself at me—I didn't have time to duck.'

'It isn't a joke, Mark!'

'I wasn't being funny. I meant that—I opened the front door to her and the next thing I knew she had her arms round my neck and was trying to kiss me.'

'And succeeding!'

'I was not kissing her, Sancha. It was all one-sided. How many times do I have to tell you?' He sat up, scowling, and she hurriedly looked away from his naked body. Leaning over, she pulled the duvet off his bed and threw it to him.

'We can't talk properly until you cover yourself up—wrap yourself in this!'

His hard eyes mocked her angrily. 'What's the matter, Sancha? Does it distract you to see me naked?'

'It makes it hard to have a serious discussion!' she admitted, flushing.

His gaze ran slowly, sensuously over her. 'It isn't exactly easy for me to concentrate, either, when you look like that.'

Her throat began to beat with a disturbing pulse. Mark smiled at her, looking satisfied, as if he could read her reaction, then got up, the muscles in his long, supple body lazily rippling as he threw his duvet back on his bed then walked over to the wardrobe to find a dressing-gown.

Sancha hurriedly took the opportunity to slide down inside her covers and pull her own duvet up to cover most of her. Mark turned, tying the belt of his dressing-gown, and threw her a dry glance.

'Feeling safer now?' He came back and sat on the edge of her bed, far too close to her. 'Do we have to have this serious discussion now, Sancha? I don't know about you, but I'm tired; this has been a long and very difficult day.'

'We keep putting off discussing you and that woman!'

'I've told you all there is to know!'

'No, Mark. I don't believe that now. I saw your face when I came down the stairs. You looked guilty— now why would you feel guilty unless you had been her lover?'

His voice was rough. 'How many times do I have to tell you? Why don't you believe me? I was never her lover, never!' He paused, frowning heavily. 'I admit I do feel guilty, though. It's all my fault—I should never have let myself drift into dating her. She believed it was serious, and I let her believe that. I liked her—a lot. I might even have fallen in love with her if we had gone on seeing each other much longer.'

'Are you sure you weren't in love?' Jealousy made her voice thick, made her throat burn.

He sighed. 'No, Sancha. If you hadn't been in the way I might have fallen in love with her, but I didn't. I even tried to make myself feel as much for her as she did for me, but I couldn't. I simply enjoyed being able to relax with her, talk about work, about the company problems. I used to talk to you about all that, but you never had time any more, and I needed to talk to someone.'

She gave him a scathing look. 'Oh, really? Funny that you picked a very sexy girl to talk to! Unless you'd secretly thought of having an affair?'

He groaned. 'How many more times do I have to tell you? I didn't! Not in the beginning. That's the trouble with love affairs. The first step is dangerously easy to take. You have dinner together, you talk about work, about your problems, and it's downhill from then on—a primrose path which can end in hell, for somebody.'

It had been hell for her ever since she'd got that anonymous letter. When had that been? She couldn't remember now. Time had no meaning any more. It seemed like weeks ago, but it could only be a matter of days.

Mark said flatly, 'Sancha, I swear to you, I didn't start out meaning to have an affair with her.'

'What did you intend, then? A meaningful friendship?' Her bitter sarcasm made his face tighten. He looked at her bleakly.

'Please believe me, Sancha. I didn't realise what I was getting myself into at first, and by the time I did realise the dangers, it was too late.'

'Too late to stop?' she asked, her face white with pain. She couldn't bear the agony of hearing him talk about what had happened between him and Jacqui Farrar, and yet she had to know; it was eating her inside, not knowing.

He ran his hands over his face as if to wipe off the tension holding his features rigid. In a low voice he muttered. 'No, not that. It's all over, I promise you that—but, Sancha, that poor girl is hurting now, because of me. That's why I feel so guilty. I should never have let it go on; I should have stopped seeing her as soon as I realised she was ... serious.'

'Yes, you should,' Sancha said, half abstractedly. She believed him; he was too serious to be lying. The trouble was she had something else to worry about now. Jacqui Farrar had screamed at her, 'You'll always know he's mine ...' And then she had said, 'I haven't finished with you yet ...'

She might merely have been making empty threats because she was hurt and angry—but what if she'd been serious? What would she be planning right now?

Mark's hands dropped; she saw his set face, his sombre eyes. He was worried about the blonde girl, too.

'She isn't giving up,' Sancha said in a voice that quivered. 'You know that. I'm scared, Mark. She's obsessed with you, you're under her skin, and obsessed people lose all sense of proportion. She might do anything.'

'Don't let your imagination run away with you!' he said, sounding very calm, but his eyes told her he was far more anxious than he wanted to admit. He knew Jacqui Farrar and what she was capable of—but he didn't want Sancha to worry about her.

'You know I'm not imagining things!' she whispered.

Mark grimaced. 'What can she do?' he said. 'So long as you and I are back together again, what can Jacqui do to hurt us?'

'I don't know, Mark,' Sancha said slowly. 'I just know she'll try.'

CHAPTER EIGHT

MARK sat in grim silence for a moment, his face taut. Sancha saw the lines on his face and the weariness in his eyes, and said anxiously, 'You look tired and so am I. Go to bed, Mark.'

He looked at her mutely, then at the other bed, with a question in his eyes that she read with no difficulty, but she shook her head. 'No. I think you'd better sleep in the spare room tonight, don't you? We need time to get over what's happened. It's too soon. We have to get to know each other again first.'

'How long do you expect me to wait?' he asked, with an undertone of anger.

'Oh, Mark, how can I set a time limit on it? We'll know when the moment comes.'

'Sancha . . .' he murmured huskily, putting out his hand.

They looked at each other in silence. He was still asking her that question, pleading without words, and Sancha found it hard to say no again. But Flora chose that moment to cry out in her sleep, and Sancha at once tensed, turning her head to listen intently.

Was Flora having one of her nightmares? But after that one little whimper silence fell again.

'She certainly knows how to pick her times!' Mark muttered, his hand dropping to his side again.

'It's difficult to talk with the children around!' Sancha said huskily. Even more difficult to enjoy lovemaking when you were constantly afraid of being interrupted by a child calling you, she thought, or, even worse, having a child running into the bedroom at the wrong moment. The need to be quiet while you were making love, the fear of being overheard by one of your children made it hard to give yourself up to passion. Hadn't that been one of the causes of their drift apart?

The state of being 'in love' didn't last for ever. It illuminated the first year or two of marriage, like a rainbow, but then daily life dimmed that light and you were usually too busy to notice what was happening.

Slowly love changed, became less intense, the excitement went and what you had left, if you were lucky, was love itself—ordinary, everyday love without the highs and lows of being 'in love'.

Maybe that's where our marriage went wrong? thought Sancha. Maybe everyday love isn't enough for Mark? He still wants that early, excited feeling?

Mark said slowly, 'We need a few days together, alone, without them. Do you think Zoe might...?'

She laughed, imagining her sister's reaction if she suggested it. 'No! Oh, no. Zoe finds them too much work, and I think she's positively scared of Flora at times.'

He pulled a face. 'Well, I'm not surprised—she scares me, too. She's a ferocious infant.'

Indignantly Sancha protested, 'How can you say that? She's a pet.'

'A pet with very messy habits. Five minutes of Flora and the house is a tip! She sits in that playpen of hers and hurls toys all over the room.'

Sancha couldn't deny that, and laughed.

'That's why she goes on doing it!' Mark said drily. 'Because you and Martha sit there laughing at her tricks.'

'Martha adores her.'

Mark looked thoughtful. 'So she does. I wonder...would *she* have her and the boys for a whole weekend?'

Sancha thought about it, her face brightening. 'She might. She enjoys having them for a few hours. And if Zoe agreed to help out—if she took the boys out on the Saturday, for instance, which I think she would do because she finds them easier to handle...'

'Your sister certainly has a way with the opposite sex,' Mark said with amusement. 'Even the little ones.'

Sancha laughed. 'She always has had! Even when we were really small I can remember the effect Zoe had on boys. They never even noticed me. I was just a neatoid schoolgirl. Zoe was the one who made their eyes pop before she even got into her teens. I never had that effect on any of the boys at school.'

'They must have been blind, then!' Mark said, looking at her through his lashes and smiling as her colour rose. 'I never looked twice at Zoe.'

Sancha remembered. It had annoyed Zoe to realise that Mark wasn't remotely interested. Sancha had been afraid he would fall for Zoe the minute he met her, as so many of Sancha's boyfriends had before him, but Mark hadn't seemed to notice Zoe at all.

'That's why she's never married, of course,' Mark said drily. 'She could never be satisfied with just one man. She likes queues of them standing in line.'

Sancha was taken aback. 'That isn't very nice, Mark. It's just that Zoe has never met the right man yet.'

He smiled at her. 'Your sister's OK, I've learnt to like her more, but I see her more clearly than you do. She's very picky, very self-centred. She's always been able to have almost any man she wants, so she can never make up her mind about any of them—she keeps hoping something better will come along.'

Sancha frowned, thinking about that and wondering if he had hit on something. It had often puzzled her that Zoe had never married and yet always had men around.

'Anyway,' Mark said, 'to get back to a more interesting subject... Will you talk to Martha and Zoe and try to get them to work out some way of taking care of the kids for a weekend?'

'Well, I might talk to them on Monday,' she said slowly, but she was a little hesitant. They had been so good already, each of them. Zoe had had Flora for half a day, and Martha had had all three children today.

Mark said eagerly, 'It would be great if Martha could have the kids next weekend, if she can manage that—the sooner the better.'

A little more colour crept up her face and she looked away from the demanding brilliance of his eyes. It would be so easy to give in now, forget what had happened with Jacqui Farrar. That was what one part of her wanted to do—badly. But another part of her knew that their marriage would only survive if they both felt the same, both wanted to make it work.

'Martha did have them today, remember,' Sancha reminded him, and he sighed.

'Well, see what she says.'

'OK.' She looked at her watch. 'I'm very tired, Mark.'

He got up, then leaned down to kiss her lightly, very softly, on the mouth.

'Goodnight, Sancha.'

'Goodnight,' she whispered, fighting to stay in control. She must not give in now.

He stood there for a few seconds, watching her, then reluctantly picked up his clothes and walked out of the room. She watched him go with longing, aching to call him back, invite him into her bed, but knowing that it was far too soon. She was too raw from discovering what had been going on, and still not quite certain Mark had not totally betrayed her.

There had been a betrayal—no question of that. He had thought, at least, of becoming Jacqui Farrar's lover, and he almost had done—and Sancha had to get over the pain of that before she could forgive and forget. How could they be happy again if her head was full of doubts and uncertainties?

But was she taking a terrible risk? She knew she would rather die than lose Mark, yet she was hesitating. Wasn't it crazy? Wasn't she risking losing him by making him wait like this? Jacqui Farrar hadn't gone away, hadn't accepted the situation—she was out there somewhere, brooding, planning her next move. *She* would never make Mark wait; she would grab him, if she could, without a second's hesitation.

Wasn't that what she, herself, ought to do?

But a marriage needed a firm bedrock of trust and love—you couldn't build a life together on anything less.

Sancha put out the light and lay in the dark listening to the silence in the house, the breathing of her family in their sleep. It satisfied something in her nature to have them all here, safely under the same roof, the man and the children who made up her world, who needed her as much as she needed them.

That was what she had forgotten for a while, since Flora's birth! She had been so fixated on the children's need for her that she had lost sight of Mark's needs, her own need for him. Now that she had remembered, she would make sure she never forgot again.

She woke up with the delicious fragrance of coffee in her nostrils, and slowly opened her drowsy eyes to find Mark sitting on her bed in morning sunlight. He was fully dressed in a sweatshirt and jeans.

Startled, Sancha sat up. 'What time is it?' Now she was wide awake, her responsibilities rushed in on her as usual. 'Flora...' she thought aloud, her eyes worried.

'Is downstairs, in her playpen,' Mark said reassuringly. 'With the boys, watching a cartoon on television. I brought you some coffee and toast. I had my breakfast with the kids.' He held out a plate with a slice of buttered toast on it and Sancha took it slowly.

'You got their breakfast?' Her eyes were wide with incredulity.

'No need to sound so surprised. I made their porridge in the microwave—the instructions were very simple, nothing blew up and, although I admit a lot of the porridge got onto Flora and her highchair, she ate quite a bit too and seemed to enjoy herself.' He looked at her, grinning. 'Eat your toast before it gets cold.'

She bit into it, suddenly hungry. Mark had drawn the curtains and the sun was streaming into the room.

She caught sight of herself in the dressing-table mirror; her tawny hair was dishevelled, her face pink from sleep, her nightdress slipping off one shoulder, leaving a lot of her pale skin bare. What *did* she look like?

Mark caught her hurried sideways glance and grinned at her. 'You look very sexy,' he murmured, reading her mind. 'I only wish I would join you.'

Her colour deepened, her breathing abruptly faster, very unsteady and ragged.

His eyes mocked her. 'But I suppose I'd better go down and keep an eye on the kids,' he said with a faint sigh. 'Or Flora will manage to break out of her playpen and do something I'll regret.'

'She would, given half a chance,' agreed Sancha, still very flushed, but smiling.

He leaned forward and kissed her bare shoulder lingeringly. The caress made her skin burn; she wanted to put her arms around his neck and pull him down onto the bed, but he had straightened a second later.

'Take your time getting up. No need for you to cook lunch—I'm taking us out. We'll go for a walk in the forest then have lunch at a pub somewhere—how about The White Swan?'

'I'd love it,' she said contentedly, and when he had gone she finished her coffee and toast, then got up and had a leisurely bath. She put on a white pleated skirt and yellow tunic top, did her make-up and hair, and went downstairs to find the kitchen spotlessly tidy, with no sign of anyone having done any cooking or having eaten breakfast.

Mark was in the sitting-room with the three children, who barely looked up, their eyes glued to the television screen. Mark looked, though, his grey eyes moving over her in a way that brought a new rush of colour to her face.

'I was afraid you might put on the everlasting jeans again!'

She laughed, shaking her head.

'Ready to go?' he asked her softly. 'We are, aren't we, kids?'

The boys jumped up in answer and switched off the television. 'Are we going? Oh, cool. Come on, Dad, let's get the car out. Oh, shut up, Flora—never mind the cartoon; we're going to the forest!'

They dashed out, both of them fully dressed in clean shirts, jeans and trainers, their hair brushed, their faces clean. Mark followed them.

'I've packed a basket with some lemonade and fruit,' he told Sancha over his shoulder. 'Come on!'

Flora held her arms out to Sancha, who lifted her up out of the playpen. Mark had dressed her in a pair of her favourite dungarees, in a coral-pink which clashed with her flame-red hair and yet looked good on her in some baffling way. Under them she wore a white sweatshirt. Her face was clean, too, and her hair was tangle-free and brushed.

Sancha couldn't get over Mark having coped so well with getting the children up, fed and dressed. He had helped her with the children in the beginning, now and then. But lately he had always been so busy, and when he wasn't working so tired, that he had simply got out of the habit of asking if he could do anything to help, and she had ceased to expect him to do anything.

How easy it was to fall into habits which set like concrete and became a seemingly unalterable routine! Day after day drifted by and you forgot there had

ever been another way of living, you lost sight of the
way things had been in the beginning. You stopped
sharing little tasks like feeding the children, washing
up, doing shopping; you stopped noticing each other;
you stopped touching, kissing, loving; you moved
apart so far that you didn't recognise each other any
more, and suddenly your marriage was in crisis and
under threat.

Had Mark seen that now? He must have done.
Wasn't that why he had taken care of the children,
got their breakfast, brought her coffee and toast in
bed? Mark had been trying to show her that he meant
to make their life together work again, in every
possible way, and she was fiercely glad to know that
that was how he felt.

Her heart was full of hope as they drove away from
their home. She couldn't even remember the last day
they had had out together, as a family. The children
were wildly excited to be going out with their father,
staring out of the car windows and chattering eagerly
as Mark headed straight out of town into the forest
which lined the old Roman road running straight as
a die for mile after mile.

Before they reached the forest they passed cottages
whose gardens were awash with flowers, with lilac and
dark blue irises, and wallflowers whose massed
orange, rust-red and yellow burnt like flames behind
the green hedges, their heady scent immensely nos-
talgic, reminding Sancha of other spring days long
ago. Her father had always had wallflowers in the
garden when she was a child. She loved that scent.

A few moments later they passed the last cottage
and were in the forest, which had been planted nine
centuries ago, during Norman times, so that the

monarch and his courtiers could hunt whenever they were in this countryside. Villages had been torn down and ordinary people dispossessed before these trees were planted and deer let loose to wander through them until the hunt began. Few people ever remembered that when they enjoyed the forest at weekends.

Sancha began to tell the boys the names of the trees they saw. Stately oak, with new, frilled green leaves, and ash, the latest to come into pale bronze leaf, and noble, towering beech, and thorn trees, and delicate, dancing hazel trees.

'They're planted close together so that they can be culled every year or so, to provide wood for garden fences, trellis work, long poles,' she told the boys, who weren't really listening.

'When can we get out to play in the forest?' they asked their father.

'Just round the next bend,' Mark said, and a few moments later slowed and parked in an off-the-road car park with a surface of trodden earth. There were already half a dozen cars parked there; the forest was a popular weekend venue. By noon the car park would be full; it always was on fine Sundays. Even in winter there were plenty of people in the forest, walking their dogs or riding.

The children all clambered out, chattering excitedly. They had brought Flora's pushchair, but she refused to get into it; she wanted to run along with the boys.

'Me walk,' she indignantly told her mother, staggering off behind her brothers, shouting for them to wait. Of course, they took no notice, and Flora yelled, red in the face. 'Wait for me!'

The boys ran faster.

'When she's tired she'll want her pushchair, so you'd better take it, anyway,' Sancha told Mark with resignation as they followed their children into the forest.

Mark took her hand and swung it as they walked, making Sancha feel years younger, reminding her of how it had been before they got married, how much fun they had had together, just the two of them. She couldn't remember the last time they had held hands as they walked.

'I think the boys should start riding on Sunday mornings soon—they're old enough,' Mark said. 'I'll drive them here.'

'They'd love that,' she agreed, but for how long would he keep it up? He often had to work at weekends, and then it would be left to her to get the boys to the riding stables.

And, of course, as soon as she heard about her brothers going riding, Flora would want to ride, too, and there would be endless scenes with her.

The forest held several open glades, whose turf was bitten down almost to the roots, grazed by the deer which one never caught sight of but which lived somewhere in the depths of trees, sleeping by day in among the brambles and tussocks of long grass, to keep out of the way of human visitors, and browsing by night when there was nobody around.

The forest glades were also rich with wild spring flowers: creeping wood sorrel, with its mauve-veined delicate white petals, yellow oxalis, which only opened out in full sunlight, clusters of blue flax, yellow birdsfoot trefoil, vetch and purple toadflax, which the children at once recognised as a relation of the snap-dragons which grew in their garden at home.

'But these are only little snapdragons,' said Felix.

'Baby ones,' agreed Charlie.

'They're the wild version,' Sancha told them.

Charlie's hand reached out, but their father said sharply, 'No, don't pick any! They'll die before you get them home, and you might damage the roots.'

'I want some!' Flora whimpered at once, tears coming into her eyes.

'You don't want them to die, do you?' Mark asked sternly.

'Love them—want some!' She reached out one small, plump hand to pick a stem of shivering blue flax, glaring at him, obstinacy in every line of her tiny body, but Mark was just as stubborn as she was.

'Don't pick it, Flora,' he said, his face set. 'Or I shall be very cross with you.'

She staggered to her mother, arms held up. 'Bad man. Bad Dadda,' she sobbed.

Sancha lifted her into her arms and patted her back, automatically making soothing noises.

'Want flower,' Flora told her. 'Mummy...want flower...'

'No, darling, you heard what Daddy said—the poor flower would die if you picked it. You don't want it to die, do you?'

Flora's wails went up an octave.

'Time for her pushchair, I think. She's obviously getting tired,' Mark murmured drily, and Sancha nodded. When Flora got tired she always became crotchety.

The two boys crashed on into the forest, whooping as they ran through new, young ferns. Sancha strapped Flora into her pushchair and Mark pushed.

'No—want to run, want to play with Charlie,' Flora shouted, kicking her legs, but her parents took no notice, walking on slowly into the shadowy forest, where sunlight flickered through new green leaves and made moving patterns on the narrow, winding paths. Flora stared up at it, fascinated, no longer yelling. Slowly her lids grew heavy and closed.

Mark took one of Sancha's hands again, his fingers entwining with hers, and her body filled with contentment.

'If the worst comes to the worst, I thought we might move further up north,' he said, swinging their linked hands between them. 'I might get a job with Harry Abbey—remember him? Big, burly chap a few years older than me, going bald the last time I saw him. He was our managing director for a couple of years before he set up on his own in Yorkshire. He gave me a ring last week, said he'd heard about our problems and that if I ever needed a job to call him first.'

'That was nice of him!' She vaguely remembered the man; he had had a rugged, kindly face.

'He's a decent guy. It isn't a big company, of course, and I wouldn't be earning anything like my present salary, but one thing I liked about the offer was that Harry said he'd want me back on the site, rather than working in an office, and that suits me. You know I love to be out on site; I was never happy in an office.'

She turned to smile at him indulgently. 'I know— so that would be great, wouldn't it?'

'But we would have to move, and Yorkshire is a long way from here. And money would be quite tight. As I say, Harry couldn't pay me anything like the amount I've been earning with Frank.'

'If you were happy, that wouldn't matter; we'd manage. I've heard that prices of property are much lower up north—we'd sell our house for a lot more than we'd have to pay for a smaller place up in Yorkshire, wouldn't we?'

'Oh, yes, that's true—I think that this time we'll buy an older, bigger property, Victorian or Edwardian, instead of a modern house. It would be cheaper, we would have more room, and I could do some work on the house myself—put in a new kitchen, modernise the bathrooms, for instance—at half the cost of having it done by someone else.'

'That would be fun,' she said, eyes bright. 'I'll help you—we can do the work together.'

His fingers tightened on her hand and he smiled down at her. 'We always used to, remember? In our first house? Remember what a mess it was when we first bought it? It took us a year to get it looking the way we wanted it.'

She remembered it vividly; they were happy memories.

Ahead of them the boys were watching squirrels leaping along branches, high above the path.

'Look, Mum, squirrels . . .' Charlie called.

'Shh...Flora's asleep, don't wake her,' Sancha told him softly.

'Let's find somewhere to play cricket,' Mark suggested. 'There's a bigger glade down that path there.'

'We haven't got bats or a ball,' Felix pointed out.

'We have,' said Mark, holding up the wicker basket he had brought with him. 'Two bats and a ball.'

The boys whooped and ran ahead to a long rec-tangle-shaped glade where others were already playing

or having picnics. Sancha took over the pushchair and
Mark strode on to join the boys. By the time Sancha
arrived the three of them had unpacked the wicker
basket, set out the bottle of lemonade, the plastic
mugs and the five apples on the grass, and were
marking out their little cricket pitch with twigs bal-
anced on top of swaying hazel stems for a wicket.
Sancha was invited to be a fielder while Mark was the
bowler. Flora was still fast asleep, so she was left in
her pushchair with a sunshade over her to keep the
sun off her face.

Felix was the first batsman to hit a ball; Charlie
kept ducking, or swung wildly and missed. Mark
patiently tried again and again, bowling his younger
son slow, easy balls which Charlie still managed to
miss every time. When the two boys were flushed and
out of breath they all sat down to have a drink and
eat an apple. Flora didn't wake up, lying back in her
pushchair with the sunshade fluttering over her head,
her face pink, her mouth wide open. Mark watched
her for a second, then grinned at Sancha.

'That's how I like her best!'

Sancha knew what he meant; Flora was exhausting. But she was worth all the trouble.

'She's adorable,' Sancha said. 'I wouldn't part with
her for a million pounds!'

Mark smiled at her. 'I know you wouldn't. Maybe
I wouldn't, either, but she's still at her best when she's
asleep!'

The sun was quite hot now, as noon approached;
the sky was a deep, burning blue and the air was full
of the drone of insects and the earthy scent of ferns
and grass. Sleepy, Sancha lay down on the grass near
the pushchair, with her head in the shade of an oak

standing on the edge of the glade, closed her eyes and drifted off into a half-doze. She heard the boys playing some sort of chase game in and out of the forest.

It had been a wonderful morning so far. For the first time in years they were happy together, her and Mark, and the three children. This was how it should be all the time. If they worked at it this was how it could be from now on! Happiness seeped through her veins.

A fly tickled her nose and she sleepily flapped it away with one hand, but it came back at once, hovering over her face, drifting over her cheek and then landing on her eyelid.

Through her lashes she saw a whiskery stem of grass and, holding it, Mark's brown fingers. He brushed the grass softly along her nose and then across her lips, the tickling sensation intensely sexy.

His dark head bent down; he lightly touched her mouth with his own and she put a hand up to clasp his neck, her lips parting and her heart beating fast.

Pleasure seeped through her veins. The warm sunlight, the drowsy forest sounds, the nearby laughter and shouts of children faded far away as the kiss deepened. Her eyes shut, Sancha stroked his cheek, imagining she was blind and trying to guess how he looked by exploring the hard line of bone from his eye socket down his cheek to the strong jaw. It was a very memorable face, once seen never forgotten.

Mark murmured passionately against her mouth, his hand clasping her waist, pulling her closer, and her body yielded as if she were boneless, but a second later the passionate trance was broken by a loud wail. Charlie had chosen that moment to fall over.

It was always poor little Charlie; he was clumsier than Felix. His howl of anguish made Sancha sit up, instantly alert, to look around for him.

'Oh, hell,' Mark groaned.

Charlie's yells woke Flora; she started up, her eyes flying open and her mouth wide open, too, giving out an eldritch shriek.

'Oh, no, not her as well!' ground out Mark, getting to his feet reluctantly.

'I hurt myself, Mum!' Charlie staggered over, clutching his calf where a bramble had scratched him.

'Oh, poor boy,' she said, kissing the place. 'Is that better?' Ignoring Mark's sardonic gaze, she dried Charlie's tears with a hankie from her pocket.

He ran off, cheerful again, to join his brother and several other boys in a noisy game, and Sancha gave Flora a drink of lemonade from her own mug. At once Flora's wails became gulping noises.

Mark watched and listened with a horrified expression. 'She's totally primitive, isn't she?'

'Shush,' Sancha said, stroking her daughter's red hair back from the scarlet little face. 'She's beautiful—aren't you, angel?'

'Angel? Mother-love is blind,' Mark said, laughing, then glanced at his watch. 'Time to go and find our lunch soon, I think, don't you?'

'I'm quite hungry,' agreed Sancha. 'It must be all this fresh air.'

'And all the emotion,' Mark drawled, eying her teasingly, watching her go pink.

The boys didn't want to abandon their game, or their new friends, but Mark began packing up everything, and a moment later took both boys off along the path back towards the car park.

Sancha followed in the rear with Flora, who pointed and exclaimed over every thing she saw, wide awake again and fascinated by leaves, butterflies, squirrels—all of life was a magic revelation to Flora. Sancha envied her excited enjoyment; how wonderful to be two years old and seeing the world for the first time.

Sancha was feeling something of the sort where Mark was concerned. She felt they were starting again, and even the idea of moving out of their comfortable home seemed almost exciting. She and Mark would be working on a new house together; the future held a warmth and hope that beckoned like a lighthouse to a storm-tossed ship.

They drove to The White Swan, which was a mile or so away, and found the car park almost full. This was a popular venue on a Sunday lunchtime, but Mark had already booked by phone, so their table was reserved for them in a quiet corner of the crowded dining-room.

Sancha ate very little because she was so busy making sure the children got fed and that Flora did not spill too much of her meal down herself.

They were on the dessert course when Sancha saw Mark stiffen, flashing a glance behind her, his hand tensing as he picked up the glass of white wine he was about to drink.

There was a large mirror behind him on the wall. Sancha looked into it and felt her blood chill as she saw Jacqui Farrar standing on the other side of the room. She seemed to be alone—at least, there was nobody with her at that moment.

Sancha wasn't the only one staring at her. Quite a few people had stopped eating to stare at her. Especially men. It wasn't surprising. The blonde girl looked ravishing in a simple tunic of blue silk, a white picture hat on her golden hair and her small feet in high-heeled white sandals.

Watching her, Sancha felt dishevelled and untidy; she had brushed her hair in the ladies' room before lunch, and tried to sponge all the grass-stains off her white skirt, had put on lip-gloss and dusted her face with powder too, but nothing could alter the fact that she had had three babies, her figure was no longer perfect and she was quite a few years older than the blonde girl. Just looking at Jacqui Farrar made her feel like a woman heading inexorably for middle age.

While Sancha was staring at her Jacqui Farrar suddenly noticed them, too. Sancha saw shock hit her, saw her face tighten, her slim, sexy body turn rigid, her eyes darken with bitter hostility. Seeing that look, Sancha bit down on her inner lip, anxiety flooding through her veins.

What bad luck had brought her to the same restaurant at the same time? This was a popular pub with people visiting the forest, true, but Jacqui Farrar didn't look as if she had been walking in the forest; she was far too elegantly dressed for that. She looked as if she was on her way to a garden party or the racetrack. What on earth had brought her here?

They had had such a happy day together as a family—the happiest time they had had for years— why did they have to run into that girl now? Just having her in the same room made Sancha miserable.

Looking at Mark's face, she knew what he was feeling—the same guilt and regret he had felt yesterday, confronted by Jacqui Farrar in their own home.

At least she can't come over here now and make a scene, thank God, Sancha thought with fierce relief. She wouldn't dare—not in such a public place, with so many people around, and not while we have our children with us.

And then she saw the blonde girl began to weave a path through the tables, heading straight for them.

CHAPTER NINE

MARK looked across the table at Sancha, frowning as he read the shock and dismay in her face.

'It's all right, no need to look as if the sky just fell in—I don't know why she's here, but I'll deal with her,' he said curtly, and a second later was on his feet and striding to meet Jacqui Farrar and head her off before she could reach their table.

'Where's Dad going?' asked Felix, looking round to stare. 'Who's that lady?'

'Oh, just someone from his office—eat your ice-cream, darling.' Sancha tried to sound calm and relaxed. The last thing she wanted to do was upset the children. She wasn't going to let anything ruin their day. They had had such a wonderful time until now; both boys had been very excited to have their father playing cricket with them, spending so much time with them. Nothing must spoil the happy memory they would take back home with them.

'I've nearly finished,' Felix said. 'Can I taste some of your choccy pudding? You haven't eaten much of it. Don't you like it?'

'Not much,' she said absently, and spooned some of the chocolate bombe into his bowl. She wasn't likely to eat it now, anyway. Her appetite had completely gone. Charlie clamoured to have some too, so she gave him the rest, but her attention was really on Mark and the blonde girl.

They stood in the centre of the room talking in low voices, their faces tense. What were they saying to each other? Jacqui Farrar was looking up into Mark's face, her hand fluttering near his arm, as if she wanted to touch him. Sancha watched with sickness in her stomach, her face feeling very cold, no doubt looking pale. She couldn't bear to see the other woman with Mark. Her hands screwed up into two tight little balls on her lap, her nails digging into her palms so hard it hurt.

Suddenly Mark took Jacqui Farrar's arm at the elbow and began propelling her out of the restaurant. Sancha stiffened—where were they going? Other guests were watching, too, staring and whispering, looking from Mark and Jacqui to Sancha and the children. Humiliated and distressed, Sancha wished she could just leave, but someone had to pay the bill and the children had not yet finished their desserts. She would have to wait for Mark to return.

But what if he didn't? Every time he was away from her now Sancha was terrified he would never come back.

She had taken her eyes off Flora for too long. A squelching noise made her look down and groan. 'Oh, no, Flora! You naughty girl!'

Flora had put her whole hand into her ice-cream and was playing with it, taking up handfuls and letting it drip through her fingers onto her dungarees where it formed large pink and green spots.

'Me paint,' she said smugly, admiring the effect with an enormous beam.

'That was a very naughty thing to do!' Sancha took the bowl away and began cleaning Flora up with the box of baby tissues she took everywhere with her when she was out with the children. She always needed them sooner or later, especially for Flora, who loved getting dirty. You had to be prepared for trouble when you had children; trouble was usually what you got.

Flora kicked violently against the chair-legs. 'Give me back—want it, want it,' she chanted, throwing herself about while trying desperately to reach the bowl of ice-cream, which Sancha had put just out of her reach.

The waiter, having observed all this from a distance, hurried over and began removing everything breakable from the table.

'Will you be having coffee, madam?' he asked coldly.

'Mine—give back,' Flora demanded, trying to grab her bowl as he picked it up.

Very flushed and furious, Sancha lifted Flora out of the chair and sat the child on her lap. 'No, thank you, no coffee. Could I have the bill, please?'

'Certainly, madam,' the waiter said with steely hauteur, and vanished, but before he came back with the bill Mark had reappeared, his face grim.

Sancha's heart lifted at the sight of him. Would she always feel this uncertainty about him from now on? She tried to read from his expression what had happened between him and Jacqui Farrar, but his eyes were hooded, his mouth a tight, straight line. His face gave very little away other than that he was angry about something, or with someone. With Jacqui Farrar?

Or with her? She swallowed a bitter taste, her throat moving convulsively. How did Mark really feel about her?

Despite everything he had said to her, that was one thing Sancha still didn't know. Did he really wish in his most secret heart that he could simply walk out on their marriage and go away with the other girl? If they'd had no children, was that what he would already have done? After all, he had never yet told her he still loved her, had he? If he did love her, why hadn't he said so?

He had said he wanted their marriage to be a real one again, and he had kept trying to make love to her, but some sixth sense buried deep inside her had kept warning her not to let him—yet. She couldn't believe or trust him entirely—not yet. She had always been a woman who worked by intuition, she trusted her instincts, and every instinct she had had told her to wait, to make certain that he was sincere before she let her own feelings surface, and, looking at Mark now, she was glad she had.

How would she feel if she had slept with him last night and then seen him look the way he did now?

'Are we having coffee?' he asked her, and she shook her head dumbly.

Mark coldly eyed Flora's kicking legs. 'Flora playing up again, I see. I'd better ask for the bill.'

'I asked for it; the waiter will be back with it in a minute. I'll see you outside,' Sancha said, getting up. She walked towards the door, carrying Flora, with the boys following her, pretending not to notice the curious stares of the other diners who had observed Mark and Jacqui Farrar earlier.

As she walked through The White Swan's large reception lobby her nerves jumped as she saw the blonde girl walking towards her. Oh, no! Was she coming back to confront Mark again?

Then she realised that Jacqui Farrar was not alone. Walking beside her with his hand under her elbow was a tall, distinguished man of around forty or so. He was wearing a smoothly cut suit, which Sancha felt must have cost a lot of money, and his dark hair was beginning to show traces of silver at the temples.

He must have been very good-looking when he was young, thought Sancha, staring; his lean, tanned face was certainly attractive now, although the most noticeable thing about him was a look of confidence verging on arrogance.

He was concentrating on Jacqui Farrar so hard that he didn't even bother to look at Sancha and the children as he walked past them, and neither did Jacqui Farrar, although Sancha knew she must have noticed them. She knew because the blonde girl averted her profile yet gave a scornful toss of her head, even though her eyes didn't so much as flick towards Sancha.

'That's the lady who talked to Daddy,' Felix said loudly. 'Who is she, Mummy?'

'Nobody,' Sancha said, without bothering to keep her tone low, and walked out into the car park, carrying Flora and making sure both boys stayed close to her. Car parks could be dangerous places. It was all too easy for a car to back out and hit a child which wasn't looking where it was going.

Mark emerged from The White Swan a few minutes later and joined them. Sancha's heart kicked as he came out. Again she tried to guess his mood from his expression, but his face was still unreadable. He must have seen Jacqui Farrar with the other man—had he been jealous? Was that the blonde girl's new tactic? Trying to make Mark jealous?

Sancha had a spare key and had already unlocked the car and strapped the children into their car seats. She bent her head and fumbled with her own belt as Mark got behind the wheel and started the engine.

Leaning forward, Sancha slid a favourite tape of children's songs into the tape player and switched it on.

'Must we?' Mark groaned.

'It will keep them quiet.'

'It will give me a headache, and toothache too—that stuff is pure saccharine!'

Flora was already joining in with a song about an elephant, roaring her own version while making flapping ear gestures with her hands and trumpeting through her nose.

'Does she have to do that right behind me? I wouldn't mind if she knew the words!' Mark said grimly as he turned out of the car park and began driving back through the forest.

'She loves it—what does it matter if she doesn't know the words?' Sancha hated it when he was so hard on Flora. She loved to see Flora throwing herself into what she did with such zest and enjoyment.

Ahead of them sunlight was filtering down through the trees and making flickering shadows on the road. It was mid-afternoon and drowsy insects kept mass-acring themselves on the windscreen. It would need to be washed tomorrow morning, she thought. She was trying to stop herself thinking about anything that could hurt.

The boys were singing now, too—it was difficult to hear anything else above their voices, but it would make sure they didn't hear what she and Mark were saying, either.

Keeping her voice low, she asked Mark, 'Who was that with Jacqui Farrar in The White Swan?'

'You saw them?' Mark shot a look at her. 'That could be her new boss—she hopes. She's applied for a job with him and is meeting him for lunch today to talk about it.'

Sancha's heart lifted, but over the last few days she had been on a switchback ride to hell and back and she no longer knew what to believe.

'Really? That was a fast change of mind. Only yesterday she refused to let you go.'

'She had no option; I made that clear last night.' Mark spoke so quietly she only just heard him, but his face was flinty with anger. 'Apparently she deliberately sent you that anonymous letter, and made that phone call, in the hope of making you angry enough to kick me out and ask for a divorce. Can you believe it? She was fed up with waiting for me to make up my mind, she said, so she forced it all out into the open. Is that scheming, or what?'

'I worked that out. That had to be her motive, and in a funny sort of way I'm glad she did it, because if she hadn't I wouldn't have found out what was going on for ages, and by then—' She broke off without saying what she was thinking, and Mark gave a rough sigh, nodding, his face sombre.

'Yes.'

They both knew that if Sancha hadn't found out that Mark was seeing Jacqui Farrar he might well have ended up in the blonde girl's bed. Sancha knew she could have forgiven him, if he'd come back to her, but it would have hurt far more.

'Well, I hope she gets this new job.' She thought about it, then asked, 'He's interviewing her on a

Sunday, over lunch in a pub? That's a funny way to interview someone for a job.'

Mark said wryly, 'Yes, isn't it?'

'I wonder what his wife will think about that, when she hears. Or isn't he married?' Was some other woman soon to start worrying about her marriage and wondering what her husband was up to with his personal assistant?

Mark shrugged. 'I don't know anything about his private life. Maybe he isn't married. And even if he is, he can no doubt do as he likes. He looked to me like a man who knows what he wants and always gets it.'

'Maybe Jacqui Farrar has met her match, then,' Sancha said, and felt great satisfaction in the thought. Sancha wouldn't care to get mixed up with a man who looked like that. He certainly wouldn't be easy to manage. Had Mark been? No, he was no push-over, either. Maybe Jacqui Farrar liked tough men; maybe she enjoyed the chase and the triumph when they surrendered?

'What business is he in, do you know?' she asked, and Mark nodded.

'His name is Thom Johannson. He's an investment manager with a big insurance firm. Our firm did some work for him—that's how Jacqui met him first. I noticed at the time that he seemed interested in her. Whenever she was around Johannson watched her. I think he's of Scandinavian descent; maybe it was her blonde hair that attracted him?'

Sancha smiled at that. 'He isn't blonde, himself, though.'

'No, I suppose he takes after his English mother. But he certainly fancied Jacqui, and she knew it. She's very streetwise and never misses it when a man keeps staring at her. I imagine that when I told her I wanted her to find a new job she rang him immediately.'

Sancha watched his long, slim hands firmly manipulating the wheel and felt her heart beating in her throat. He didn't sound as if his heart was broken. Or even dented a little. He didn't sound like a man in love who was saying goodbye to a dream. His tone when he spoke about Jacqui Farrar had been dry and slightly cynical, if anything, but without pain or anger.

'Are you OK?' she asked him in a whisper, and he shot her another sideways look, frowning, then smiled at her, a flash of a smile that left her breathless.

'If you're asking what I think you're asking, then just wait and let me show you tonight,' he whispered back, and she couldn't halt the relentless tide of hot colour rising in her face, the rapid beating of the pulse in her neck.

Mark saw it, his eyes narrowed and passionate, then he looked back at the road and drove in silence for a long time while Sancha leaned back in her seat and gave herself up to a deep happiness, her eyes closing and her body limp with relief.

She was no longer even aware of the bouncy music coming from the loudspeakers in the car, or of the children in the back, singing along with it. All she knew was that Jacqui Farrar was soon going to be out of Mark's life for good and their marriage had another chance; she and Mark could begin again. Mark belonged to her—she would never again let anything come between them, not even their children.

When they got back to the house they put the children in front of one of their favourite cartoons and went into the kitchen to start preparations for teatime. First, though, Sancha made a pot of tea and poured them both a cup which they sat at the kitchen table to drink.

'It was an odd coincidence, her turning up at The White Swan when we were there, wasn't it?' she thought aloud, and Mark made a grimace.

'You may not believe this, but it *was* a pure co-incidence, Sancha. I hadn't told her we would be there.'

Their eyes met and she smiled at him, her brown eyes glowing. 'I believe you—I could see from her face that she was startled to see us there.'

'Being right out of town makes The White Swan a place people often choose for very private rendezvous,' said Mark. 'Although heaven knows why—it's always crowded.'

'It's romantic, though. Very old and right in the middle of the forest. I love it.' She paused, then asked quietly, 'But what were you two arguing about in the restaurant before you hurried her out of there?'

'I asked her to wait for Thom Johannson in the bar, and to leave us alone, and she flew into a temper. I had to hustle her out of the room. It wasn't a very pleasant moment. I was furious with her for causing trouble again, and I was afraid she might make a big scene in front of the children.'

Sancha shivered. 'That was what I was afraid of, too!'

Mark watched her anxiously. 'I could see you were. I saw the look on your poor, worried little face the minute she walked in—and it made me hate myself.' He paused, then said huskily, 'Darling, forgive me for what I've done to you. I can't make excuses. Oh,

I know I did, I know I told you it was all your fault—
and that must have hurt you even more.'

'You weren't wrong, though,' Sancha said at once.
'It wouldn't have happened if I hadn't let us drift
apart.'

'But it takes two, Sancha. Because of the problems
we've been having at work this year I started to feel
as if I was the only one in trouble, but I wasn't, was
I? You had problems, and I knew that. You'd had a
bad time when you were carrying Flora, the birth was
difficult, and then you had Flora herself. Now that
I've been with her for a whole day I can only admire
your patience with her; she's exhausting.'

'She's a terrible drain on me, but, as I said, I
wouldn't part with her for a million pounds,' Sancha
told him, and he laughed shortly.

'I know you adore her, but she is tiring, Sancha. I
think you should send her to a nursery school for a
few hours a week—it would give you time to yourself,
and take some of the burden off you.'

'I have considered the idea,' she admitted. 'Maybe
next year, when she's just that bit older.'

'You need time away from her, Sancha,' he said,
very seriously. 'Time for yourself, time to get more
rest.'

'She needs me. Kids like Flora need all the love they
can get, and they do give it back, Mark, she's a very
affectionate little girl. I'll carry on for another year.
Until she's at least three.'

He gave her a resigned look. 'Stubborn as a mule,
aren't you? OK, so long as you don't overtire yourself.
The boys need you, too, you know, and so do I. Please
don't push me to the back of the queue for your attention again.'

'I won't,' she promised, looking into his eyes.

He held out his hand and she put her fingers into it, feeling the strength of his grip tighten. 'I should have talked to you long ago,' he whispered. 'Told you how I felt, made you understand what was happening to us, but instead I sulked. I felt neglected and unhappy, so instead of trying to talk it out with you I went elsewhere for comfort. I realise I hurt you badly, and I wish to God I hadn't done it. If I could turn the clock back, believe me, I would, and I promise you it will never happen again, but please, please, make more room for me in your life, Sancha.'

She lifted his hand to her lips, kissed the palm slowly, deeply, inhaling the scent of his skin.

'You've always been the most important part of my life—don't you know that? I just lost sight of that for a while because I was so snowed under with the kids, but it was always true. I love you, Mark.'

Mark's breathing seemed to still. 'Sancha...' he whispered, staring at her with darkened, intent eyes, and she smiled at him with quivering, passionate lips.

'There will always be room for you in my life, and in future we'll make sure we talk to each other, say what's on our minds, in our hearts. That's what we should have done all along, Mark, you're right.'

'That was my fault!' he muttered, his face shadowed.

'No,' she protested. 'Don't you see—we were both to blame! I didn't talk to you, either. I lost sight of you because I was so busy; I even forgot I loved you. We lost touch with each other. But all that is over now, that's the important thing, and we're together again. We must learn from what's happened, and in future we must always tell each other honestly how we feel!'

'I can tell you how I feel right now,' he said, getting up and coming round the table to lift her from her chair.

She looked up at him, her heartbeat deafening her.

Mark held her gaze, his face passionate. 'If we didn't have the kids in the house I'd take you upstairs right now and show you!'

She put her fingers on his lips. 'Shh...walls have ears in this house! Little tiny ears, but very sharp ones.'

His mouth moved against her fingertips, kissing them. 'We must somehow get someone to agree to move in here and look after the kids while we go away for a few days.'

'I'll talk to Martha and Zoe tomorrow,' she promised.

Mark kissed her, his arms going round her waist and the demand of his mouth forcing her head back. 'It has to be soon, darling,' he groaned against her mouth. 'I'm getting desperate.'

From the doorway they heard heavy breathing, and broke apart. The two boys stared at them, scandalised.

'I thought you were watching TV,' Mark said, glaring.

'Flora has gone to sleep in her playpen,' Felix said.

'Good—don't wake her up,' Mark said.

'Aren't you going to put her to bed?' Charlie asked, eyes round as saucers.

'Let sleeping Floras lie, as your Auntie Zoe says,' Sancha told him. 'It's nearly teatime, anyway. You can help me lay the table, then when tea is ready I'll go and wake Flora up.'

There was no need to do that. Flora woke up five minutes later, and began shouting as soon as she discovered she was alone and the television had been switched off.

She was hungry again, amazingly, considering how much she had eaten at The White Swan. She had a boiled egg with soldiers of toast to dip into it, some yoghurt and a few cherries, with orange juice to drink.

Watching Sancha lifting her out of her highchair later, Mark asked, 'How does she manage to get half her food on herself every time she eats anything?'

'Her hand and eye co-ordination isn't perfect yet,' Sancha said defensively, wiping her face and hands.

'She likes making a mess,' said Felix.

'That's what *I* worked out,' his father told him, grinning at him.

Sancha carried Flora off to bed, already drowsy, and the boys followed them reluctantly. It took an hour to get them all settled. Sancha told the boys a story about a space monster coming to earth to find electric pylons to eat, then put out the light and tiptoed away, leaving them half-asleep. By then Flora was dead to the world.

She was surprised to find Mark in the kitchen—he turned from the oven, an apron tied around his waist and wearing a triumphant grin, with a plate in each oven-gloved hand.

'I cooked our supper!'

He had sometimes cooked this meal when he and Sancha had first met, all those years ago. It had been his standby on evenings when he was eating alone in his one-room flat, or when he couldn't afford to take her out to a restaurant. It was a simple meal, but delicious—spaghetti with a quickly made sauce of tomatoes, peppers, mushrooms and onions. Over each plate he had thrown curls of freshly shaved Parmesan cheese and sprigs of parsley.

He hadn't cooked for her for ages, though. 'It looks wonderful,' Sancha said, admiring the kitchen table, laid for two, with candles in the centre and glasses of red wine already poured out. 'Very romantic!'

'That's the big idea,' he said, laying the plates on the table and looking round at her with half-closed, smouldering eyes. 'I'm getting you in the right mood. In case you hadn't noticed.'

Her pulses skipped. Of course she had noticed. Did he think she was blind?

Mark's narrowed eyes observed with unhidden amusement the rise of colour in her face, but he didn't say anything, turning to put on some soft music and switch off the electric light. They ate by candlelight, talking very little. Sancha's heart was beating like a drum all the time, almost drowning out the music. When they had finished the meal they piled everything they had used into the dishwasher, then Mark leaned over the table, blew out the candles, turned off the music and took her hand.

'I can't wait any longer, Sancha,' he whispered, his eyes glittering with a desire that made every hair on the back of her neck prickle with response. 'Come to bed.'

Silently she went with him, and as they climbed the stairs the house around them was full of gentle, quiet breathing from the rooms where the children slept, exhausted by their day out. Don't wake up and call me! Sancha thought. Not tonight, my darlings. Sleep through till morning, for once. They might, they just

might, because they had had such an energetic day—
even Flora was worn out.

Mark didn't put on the light; he just closed their
own door as she walked past him into the room. She
heard the click of the latch, her heart leaping into her
throat, and stood there in the dark and silence,
thinking only that at last they were alone.

Mark came up behind her and her pulses jumped
with awareness of him. He slid his arms around her
waist and held her tightly, his face against her hair,
his warm breath on her nape. 'Oh, God, Sancha, if
you only knew how much I need you,' he murmured,
one of his hands moving upwards from her waist to
caress her breast, sending waves of intense pleasure
through her whole body.

She needed him, too; with a long sigh she yielded
her body up to him, her eyes closing, leaning back
against him and feeling the warmth of his flesh
reaching her through her clothes.

'I've missed you so much. I've been going out of
my mind with frustration over these months,' Mark
whispered unsteadily, his lips hot as they moved
against her neck. 'I felt so lonely without you. I love
you, darling.'

'Me, too,' she said huskily, turning in his arms to
face him, her arms going round his waist.

She felt his back muscles tense under her hands,
and heard the intake of his breath. 'Say it, then,' he
muttered. 'Tell me you love me. I badly need to hear
you say it. All this time I've felt so shut out—I felt
you'd turned your back on me, no longer needed me.
I was as miserable as sin, darling.'

Her heart hurt inside her. Had he really been so
unhappy? Oh, why hadn't she noticed? Why hadn't

she realised how he was feeling? How could she have been so blind? Oh, she herself had had a bad time, had been totally absorbed in Flora, in her housework, in caring for their children—but she should have noticed Mark's unhappiness. She couldn't forgive herself for failing to see what was happening to him.

'I'm so sorry, Mark. I didn't even realise you weren't happy, I was so busy all the time, but I love you—of course I love you—I've always loved you,' she said, her head tilting back, her eyes in the moonlight clouded with passion as she looked up at him.

'Keep saying that, keep telling me—I need to know,' he said, his voice unsteady and his grey eyes glittering. Then his mouth came down to take fierce possession of hers, his hands pulling her closer, holding her so tightly she could barely breathe.

Her head swam; her arms went round his neck and clung. Without taking his mouth from hers, Mark lifted her into his arms and began to walk towards the bed.

As he laid her down he muttered, 'First thing tomorrow we're going out to buy a new double bed; I've had enough of sleeping alone. I need you in my bed, Sancha, where I can touch you, hold you—every night, all night. That's what marriage is about, after all.'

'Yes, darling,' she whispered huskily, her blood singing in her ears as he stood up and began pulling off his clothes with hands that visibly trembled. She knew how he felt; the same urgency was eating at her.

She sat up and started undressing, dropping her clothes on the floor like a teenager, but went on watching him as if her life depended on it. In a way, it did; she needed to see him, to remind herself of what she had been missing for so long: the long, powerful body, roughened by dark hair, the deep chest and flat stomach, the strong hips and the muscled thighs. Mark had a beautiful body.

Her lethargy, her lack of desire, her reluctance to be touched throughout all those months since Flora's birth were far away in the past. The other night she had seen him naked again for the first time in months and had been taken by surprise by her own body's reaction, by the agonising sting of desire. She felt the same now. She wanted to look, to touch, to caress him, and from the way Mark stared back she knew he felt the same.

His eyes were so full of heat they were almost molten, flickering from her full, bare breasts, with their aroused pinky-brown nipples, over her smooth, pale hips and to the thighs below them. He had shed the last of his clothes; so had she. For a second or two they didn't move, just looked at each other, desire burning the air between them.

Then Mark suddenly knelt down in front of her, stark naked, and leaned his face forward to kiss her breasts. Shivering with need, Sancha stroked his tousled black hair, combing it back with her fingers from his flushed face. His hair clung to her fingertips; she almost felt she saw sparks of electricity coming from the wiry strands.

'Darling,' he muttered, his lips parting around one of her nipples. 'You're so beautiful, Sancha. Even lovelier than you were when I met you.'

His mouth slid down slowly, kissing every inch of her midriff, his tongue sliding round and round inside her navel, then on again, even lower, sending feverish shudders through her as he nuzzled her bare knees apart. By then Mark was breathing as if he had just run a mile.

His skin was hot between her thighs, his head moving inward, making her catch her breath with intense sensuality as he found what he was seeking. She seemed to be so weak with desire she was boneless, melting. She shut her eyes, groaning hoarsely, her hands sliding down the powerful line of his back, following the indentations of his spine to the curve of his buttocks.

The moist heat of his tongue was driving her crazy. She buried her face in his bare shoulder, her mouth open, whimpering with pleasure, her teeth grazing his skin as passion beat up inside her like wind-driven flame.

'Yes... Oh, Mark...darling...I love you,' she gasped, tasting the saltiness of his hot skin.

Suddenly he rolled her backwards onto the bed and fell on top of her with a rough cry of urgency. She arched instinctively, her arms round him, holding him, pushing him down into her, meeting the thrust of his flesh with a wild gasp of satisfaction.

They were in such a hurry to end the long frustrations they had suffered that a second later they were making love, their hunger for each other an unbearable ache, stripping them of all the pride and rage and resentment that had kept them apart for too long. Moonlight flickered like lightning around them, giving them glimpses of each other every so often: his strong neck, his shoulders, the muscled thighs moving down on her, his face hot with blood, set with desire, and her mouth full and swollen with his kisses, her eyes glimmering with passion.

That long pent-up need had total possession of them both now. They weren't thinking, or even aware of anything but each other. The storm building up inside their bodies was too violent for anything else to matter. When it finally broke Sancha felt she was breaking, too, breaking into pieces, shuddering helplessly in a wild spiral of feeling too sharp and piercing to be purely pleasure, the bones of her face hurting because they were so rigid, so gripped in a spasm of pain and release, holding onto Mark, who held onto her as if he were a drowning man afraid to let go of his one chance of life. Instinctively, so as not to wake the sleeping children, they stifled their groaning cries of pleasure on each other's bodies, shuddering down through circles of satisfaction that seemed to go on and on and on for ever.

When they finally hit the bottom of that deep abyss Mark collapsed on top of her and lay there, his face buried between her breasts, breathing roughly, his chest shuddering, his body trembling, his skin so hot she felt the heat coming off him in waves.

Sancha lay slackly under him, limp as seaweed, her arms and legs flung wide apart, her eyes shut, too exhausted to speak or move.

At last Mark whispered against her perspiring skin, 'My God, I needed that!' He turned his face sideways and lightly kissed her nipple. 'I love you, Sancha. Don't ever shut me out again, will you? Promise?'

'Yes,' she groaned languidly, then lifted a hand to stroke his tousled hair. 'I love you, Mark. I promise we'll never lose each other again.'

If she had lost Mark she knew the rest of her life would have been dark and empty without him. From now on she would make sure she never lost sight of

Mark's need for her, or her need of him. What else did marriage mean? Sharing your life with someone, taking care of each other, loving each other—marriage was a two-way road. You both had to work at it. She held him tightly, enjoying the feel of his body on her, the weight of him anchoring her into their life together.

'I love you,' she said again, and lifted her mouth for his kiss.

HARLEQUIN PRESENTS®

Let passion lead the way, in our exciting series:

—when passion knows no reason...

Don't miss these dramatic stories about women who dare to risk it all for love.

August 1997—
DECEIVED (#1901)
by Sara Craven

September 1997—
THE HEAT OF PASSION (#1908)
by Lynne Graham

October 1997—
THE MARRIAGE WAR (#1913)
by Charlotte Lamb

Available wherever Harlequin books are sold.

Every month there's another title from one
of your favorite authors!

October 1997
Romeo in the Rain by Kasey Michaels
When Courtney Blackmun's daughter brought home Mr. Tall,
Dark and Handsome, Courtney wanted to send the young
matchmaker to her room! Of course, that meant the single
New Jersey mom would be left alone with the irresistibly
attractive Adam Richardson....

November 1997
Intrusive Man by Lass Small
Indiana's Hannah Calhoun had enough on her hands taking
care of her young son, and the last thing she needed was a
man complicating things—especially Max Simmons, the
gorgeous cop who had eased himself right into her little boy's
heart...and was making his way into hers.

December 1997
Crazy Like a Fox by Anne Stuart

Moving in with her deceased husband's—*eccentric*—family
in Louisiana meant a whole new life for Margaret Jaffrey and
her nine-year-old daughter. But the beautiful young widow
soon finds herself seduced by the slower pace and the much-
too-attractive cousin-in-law, Peter Andrew Jaffrey....

**BORN IN THE USA: Love, marriage—
and the pursuit of family!**

Available at your favorite retail outlet!

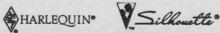

BUSA3

HARLEQUIN WOMEN KNOW ROMANCE WHEN THEY SEE IT.

And they'll see it on **ROMANCE CLASSICS**, the new 24-hour TV channel devoted to romantic movies and original programs like the special **Harlequin®** Showcase of Authors & Stories.

The **Harlequin®** Showcase of Authors & Stories introduces you to many of your favorite romance authors in a program developed exclusively for Harlequin® readers.

Watch for the **Harlequin®** Showcase of
Authors & Stories series beginning in the
summer of 1997.

If you're not receiving ROMANCE CLASSICS,
call your local cable operator or satellite provider
and ask for it today!

Escape to the network of your dreams.

1998

SUNDAY   MONDAY   TUESDAY   WEDNESDAY   THURSDAY   FRIDAY   SATURDAY

Keep track of important dates

Three beautiful and colorful calendars that celebrate some of the most popular trends in America today.

Look for:

Just Babies—a 16 month calendar that features a full year of absolutely adorable babies!

1998 CALENDAR
Just Babies
16 months of adorable bundles of joy!

Hometown Quilts
1998 Calendar
A 16 month quilting extravaganza!

Hometown Quilts—a 16 month calendar featuring quilted art squares, plus a short history on twelve different quilt patterns.

Inspirations—a 16 month calendar with inspiring pictures and quotations.

Inspirations
A 16 month calendar that will lift your spirits and gladden your heart

Steeple Hill™

◆HARLEQUIN®

Value priced at $9.99 U.S./$11.99 CAN., these calendars make a perfect gift!

Available in retail outlets in August 1997.   CAL98

Don't miss these Harlequin favorites
by some of our bestselling authors! Act now and
receive a discount by ordering two or more titles!

HT#25720	A NIGHT TO REMEMBER	$3.50 U.S.	☐
	by Gina Wilkins	$3.99 CAN.	
HT#25722	CHANGE OF HEART	$3.50 U.S.	☐
	by Janice Kaiser	$3.99 CAN.	
HP#11797	A WOMAN OF PASSION	$3.50 U.S.	☐
	by Anne Mather	$3.99 CAN.	
HP#11863	ONE-MAN WOMAN	$3.50 U.S.	☐
	by Carole Mortimer	$3.99 CAN.	
HR#03356	BACHELOR'S FAMILY	$2.99 U.S.	☐
	by Jessica Steele	$3.50 CAN.	
HR#03441	RUNAWAY HONEYMOON	$3.25 U.S.	☐
	by Ruth Jean Dale	$3.75 CAN.	
HS#70715	BAREFOOT IN THE GRASS	$3.99 U.S.	☐
	by Judith Arnold	$4.50 CAN.	
HS#70729	ANOTHER MAN'S CHILD	$3.99 U.S.	☐
	by Tara Taylor Quinn	$4.50 CAN.	
HI#22361	LUCKY DEVIL	$3.75 U.S.	☐
	by Patricia Rosemoor	$4.25 CAN.	
HI#22379	PASSION IN THE FIRST DEGREE	$3.75 U.S.	☐
	by Carla Cassidy	$4.25 CAN.	
HAR#16638	LIKE FATHER, LIKE SON	$3.75 U.S.	☐
	by Mollie Molay	$4.25 CAN.	
HAR#16663	ADAM'S KISS	$3.75 U.S.	☐
	by Mindy Neff	$4.25 CAN.	
HH#28937	GABRIEL'S LADY	$4.99 U.S.	☐
	by Ana Seymour	$5.99 CAN.	
HH#28941	GIFT OF THE HEART	$4.99 U.S.	☐
	by Miranda Jarrett	$5.99 CAN.	

(limited quantities available on certain titles)

TOTAL AMOUNT	$ _____
DEDUCT: 10% DISCOUNT FOR 2+ BOOKS	$ _____
POSTAGE & HANDLING	$ _____
($1.00 for one book, 50¢ for each additional)	
APPLICABLE TAXES*	$ _____
TOTAL PAYABLE	$ _____

(check or money order—please do not send cash)

To order, complete this form and send it, along with a check or money order for the total above, payable to Harlequin Books, to: **In the U.S.:** 3010 Walden Avenue, P.O. Box 9047, Buffalo, NY 14269-9047; **In Canada:** P.O. Box 613, Fort Erie, Ontario, L2A 5X3.

Name: _____

Address: _____ City: _____

State/Prov.: _____ Zip/Postal Code: _____

*New York residents remit applicable sales taxes.
Canadian residents remit applicable GST and provincial taxes.

Look us up on-line at: http://www.romance.net

HBKOD97